Bad Dreams
and Other Stories

Bad Dreams
and Other Stories

Tessa Hadley

JONATHAN CAPE
LONDON

1 3 5 7 9 10 8 6 4 2

Jonathan Cape, an imprint of Vintage Publishing,
20 Vauxhall Bridge Road,
London SW1V 2SA

Jonathan Cape is part of the Penguin Random House group of companies
whose addresses can be found at global.penguinrandomhouse.com

Penguin
Random House
UK

First published by Jonathan Cape in 2017

'An Abduction', 'The Stain', 'One Saturday Morning', 'Experience',
'Bad Dreams', 'Under the Sign of the Moon' and 'Silk Brocade'
all first appeared in the *New Yorker*. 'Deeds not Words' was written
for BBC Radio broadcast, 'Flight' first appeared in *Prospect* magazine,
and 'Her Share in Sorrow' was in the *Guardian* magazine.

www.vintage-books.co.uk

A CIP catalogue record for this book is available from the British Library

ISBN 9781910702888

Typeset in India by Thomson Digital Pvt Ltd, Noida, Delhi

Printed and bound by Clays Ltd, St Ives PLC

Penguin Random House is committed to a sustainable future for our business,
our readers and our planet. This book is made from Forest Stewardship
Council® certified paper.

To Julia Green

Contents

An Abduction

Jane Allsop was abducted when she was fifteen, and nobody noticed. This happened a long time ago, in Surrey, in the 1960s, when parents were more careless. She was home from boarding school for the summer, and day after day the sun rose into a cloudless sky, from which Jane couldn't unfix the word 'cerulean', which she'd learned in the art room. (She wasn't clever or literary, and was nervous of new words, which seemed to stick to her.) 'Cerulean' was more of a blank, baking glare than mere merry blue. It prised its way each morning like a chisel through the crack between Jane's flowered bedroom curtains and between the eyelids she squeezed tightly shut in an effort to stay inside her dreams. It wasn't acceptable in Jane's kind of family to complain about good weather, yet the strain of it told on them, parents and children: they were remorselessly cheerful, while secretly they longed for rain. Jane imagined herself curled up with a bag of liquorice beside a streaming windowpane, reading about the Chalet School.

But her mother said it was a crime to stay indoors while the sun shone, and Jane couldn't read outside with the same absorption; there was always some strikingly perfect speckled insect falling onto your page like a reminder (of what? of itself), or a root nudging into your back, or stinging ants inside your shorts.

The morning of the abduction, Mrs Allsop – dishevelled in a limp linen shirtdress – was wielding her secateurs up a ladder, pruning the climbing roses. She was immensely capable; tall and big-boned with a pink, pleasant face and dry yellow hair chopped sensibly short. Jane admired her mother greatly, especially when she transformed herself at night, for a concert in London or a Rotary Club dinner, with clip-on pearl earrings and lipstick and scent, a frilled taupe satin stole. Jane coveted this stole and tried it on when her mother was at the shops, making sultry faces at herself in the mirror – although sultry was the last thing her mother was, and everyone told Jane that she looked just like her. She certainly seemed to have her mother's figure, with not much bust, no waist to speak of, and a broad flat behind.

— Why don't you call up some of your old friends? Mrs Allsop suggested from the ladder top. — Invite them round to play ping-pong.

Jane responded with evasive enthusiasm. (She didn't know her old friends any more; that was what happened when you were sent away to boarding school.) She said she was heading inside to find her Jokari set (a rubber ball attached by a long elastic string to a wooden base – you could hit the ball back and forth with a paddle all by yourself for hours on end). It was part of the family code that sport and physical exercise were meaningful ways of passing leisure time; without them, you risked dissipation, letting value slip away. Only Jane's brother, Robin, was allowed a special dispensation, because he was studying to get into Oxford – it was all right for him to have his head stuck in a book all day and to go around scowling, complaining that the sun gave him headaches. When Jane strayed into Robin's room (— Buzz off, shrimp, you're not permitted across my threshold), he was curled up on his side on the bed, his clasped hands between his drawn-up knees, his glasses off, and his book propped across his face, Pink Floyd playing subduedly on the stereo. It was obvious that he'd been smoking. Mrs Allsop smoked, with a casual elegance that startled Jane, but only on the silk-stole evenings, or if she had women friends round for tea. (For Robin, blind on his bed with a headache and sex fantasies and short-circuiting flashes of insane ambition, his sister, mutely protesting – she simply stood there till he got up and pushed her out and locked the door behind her – was a visitant from his insipid past, when they'd been friends.)

Jane was listless, her mind a blank with vivid little jets of dissatisfaction firing off in it. Real children, somewhere, were wholesomely intent on untying boats or building dams or collecting butterflies to asphyxiate in jars (as she and Robin had done one summer). She should be like them, she reproached herself; or she should be more thoroughly embarked on her teenage self, like some of the girls at school, painting on make-up then scrubbing it off, nurturing crushes on friends' brothers she'd only ever seen from a distance, cutting out pictures of pop stars from *Jackie* magazine. Jane knew that these girls were ahead of her in the fated trek towards adulthood, which she had half learned about in certain coy biology lessons. Yet theirs seemed also a backward step into triviality, away from the thing that this cerulean day – munificent, broiling, burning across her freckled shoulders, hanging so heavily on her hands – ought to become, if only she knew better how to use it.

She carried the Jokari set down through the patch of woodland towards the bottom of the garden. Her sister Frances, dark-skinned and fey, not at all like their mother and not yet old enough for boarding school, had chums over to play. They were supposed to be clearing the drive of rabbit droppings with spoons and plastic bags, for money, but they were all four hunkered in a semicircle under the pine trees, where they had set out tea things for their dolls, a pine cone on each tiny plate, a rabbit dropping in each tiny cup. Jane heard Frances chanting in two alternating voices while the others watched, in thrall to her.

— Don't want it! Don't want it! Frances said in her whiny voice.

— Eat it up, her vicious voice replied. — Take your nasty medicine.

When Jane came near, the little girls melted into the undergrowth, glaring at her, hostile. She kicked their dolls over and hurled the pine cones as far as she could towards the flaunting patches of sky between the treetops (she had a strong throw, her father always said, better than Robin's); but she lacked conviction even in her malevolence. — We hate her! She's so ugly, the witch-children hummed, drifting between the bald pine trunks, keeping out of sight. Jane remembered, as she often did, how once at a friend's house she had overheard the dotty grandmother asking too loudly who the 'plain' one was. The witches didn't even bother to follow her, to spy on her, which would at least have been some kind of game. She set up her Jokari on a scorched patch of grass beside where their chalky drive debouched onto the road. No cars passed. The road was a dead end, leading only to more big houses like theirs, secretive behind their screens of trees, some atmospheric with the half-timbering that Jane didn't yet know was a badge of inauthenticity, some with tennis courts from which the thwack of balls didn't often come.

Kicking off her flip-flops, she settled resignedly into her game. The pock and thud of the Jokari ball on the baked ground soothed her, and she started to care about whether she could break her own record of consecutive hits. (She had passed Robin's record long ago.) Rapt, she didn't notice her father steering the Rover down the drive, on his way out to pick up the Saturday paper; to save petrol, he liked to roll down with the handbrake off, starting the engine only when he turned into the road. Jane scooped low to the ground under an awkward shot, getting it up with too much force just as the sleek black of the car eased into the edge of her vision; the ball on its elastic must have seemed smashed deliberately and vindictively against the car's side window (which luckily was not open). Assaulted amid his reverie, Mr Allsop was outraged out of all proportion to the offence – nothing was broken. He stopped the car and half stood up out of it to rant across its roof at Jane: Stupid girl! Didn't she have anything better to do? Then the car rolled on, ominously firing to life when it felt the road, and Jane was left wounded, staring after it. The wings of her spirit, which had been beginning to soar, faltered and flung her to earth, because, after all, she had been doing her best, nothing else; and also because her father was supposed to be her ally in the family, though they weren't at all alike. Mr Allsop was small and dark like Frances, easily bored, and clever with figures. He thought about Jane vaguely, through a fog of fond concern, fearing that she had her mother's flat, bland surface without Mrs Allsop's force of conviction.

Jane dropped her paddle in an uncharacteristic gesture of despair. Tears stung her eyes; she stood with her hands by her sides, palms outward, in a kind of resigned openness. What next, then, if even her attempt at virtue had failed?

And that was how they first saw her. They passed Mr Allsop in the Rover; he was turning out of the unmade-up road just as they turned into it. Mr Allsop noticed them, because he knew most of the cars that visited the road, and he didn't recognise or much like the look of this one: an expensive dark green sporty two-seater convertible, with one long-haired youth in a sloppy vest lolling in each seat, and one – smoking something that might have been more sinister than a cigarette – squeezed into the little luggage space behind, craning forward, as he was bound to, between his friends. The driver, who had one languid hand on the wheel, cornered carelessly in a puff of chalk dust, tyres spitting loose stones. (If they were my kids, Mr Allsop thought, catch me allowing them anywhere near my car. It's not all bad that Robin's such a drip.) Had the family ever realised that Jane had been abducted, her father would probably have remembered and suspected these visiting aliens.

The boys were drunk and stoned, and hadn't been to bed at all the night before (but then they hadn't got up until four the previous afternoon). They were out looking for girls, in Nigel's father's car. (Nigel was the one squeezed into the luggage space.) They'd finished their second year at Oxford and were staying at Nigel's house, about a twenty-minute drive from the Allsops', while his parents were away in France. After sagging at dawn, dozing in the angular Swedish armchairs in the lounge, and filling Nigel's mother's fashionable ashtrays while listening to the Grateful Dead, all three had found a second wind, swimming several thrashing lengths in Nigel's pool. The loveliness of the morning had then seemed their own fresh discovery: the light as limpid as the water, birdsong skimming the flat echoless air, the sun's touch intricate on their skin. They had decided that they needed to find girls to crown the day. That was a few hours ago. It had taken them a while to get started;

and then there'd been a striking absence, everywhere they'd driven, of available girls.

— She'll do, one of them called out when they saw Jane, loud enough for her to hear. It was Paddy (not Irish at all), the bulky, clever-looking one in the passenger seat, with small eyes like chinks of bright glass and greasy hair the colour and texture of old rope, pushed behind pink ears. He took the joint from Nigel and blinked at Jane through its smoke with a sort of appraising impartial severity, not lascivious.

— But where will we put these girls? Nigel asked facetiously, after one glance at Jane: he didn't fancy sharing his small space (and wasn't, in fact, much interested in girls). Paddy explained that they'd have to collect them one at a time.

Jane stood barefoot, hands still open in that gesture of self-relinquishment. She wasn't plain in that moment, though she didn't know it. Something was revealed in her that was normally hidden: an auburn light in her face, her freckles startling as the camouflage of an animal, blotting up against her lips and eyelids. There were ginger glints, too, in her hair, which she wore in two bunches, fastened with different-coloured elastic bands. Her eyes with their pale lashes, because she was unhappy, communicated keenly. Her family called her pudgy, but she just looked soft, as if she were longing to nestle. Her jawline was pure, the pale lips rather full, cracked, parted. She seemed not fake or stuck-up – and, just then in the dappled light, not a child either. None of this was wasted on the boys.

It didn't occur to Jane that the car would stop for her; she watched it hungrily, sifting the silky dust between her toes. Daniel, the driver, Jane saw at once, was the best-looking of the three; in fact, he was crushingly beautiful – his features smudged and vivid at once, as if sketched in black ink – and her heart fastened on him. When he had stopped the car, he asked her what her name was and she told him. — Want to come for a ride? he said kindly.

She hesitated only for a moment.

— Not in the back, she said, quite clear about it. Already, she didn't care for Nigel.

— Between us in the front, Paddy said, squeezing over.

And so she climbed in, carrying her flip-flops in her hand. On a whim, she had decided against shorts that morning; she was wearing a washed-out old dress in flowered cotton, with a Peter Pan collar.

On their way back to Nigel's house, Jane was an accomplice in an episode of shoplifting – which fortunately went undetected, or at least unreported. She had never stolen anything before; the possibility hadn't crossed her mind. But she was disorientated: as they drove along, Paddy had pulled the elastic bands off her two bunches so that her hair blew crazily into all their faces. Whipping across her vision, the strands of it were like a hallucination, distracting her from her larger bewilderment at half sitting on Paddy's knee, feeling Daniel ease his arm around her once, on a straight stretch when he wasn't changing gears. (Nigel's father had chosen a manual gearbox on the MGC.) — It's all right, Daniel had said. — Don't worry about us. We're not all bad.

— I like her, Paddy commented. — She doesn't talk too much.

The oddest thing was that she wasn't worrying, although she knew she ought to be; especially when they made plans to keep the shopkeeper talking while she, Jane, slipped bottles of whatever alcohol she could get into their canvas haversack. — He keeps it in a little side room, Daniel said. — You don't look as if you drink, so no one will suspect you. If they do, you can cry and say that we kidnapped you and made you do it.

Jane didn't recognise the shop, though it was only a few miles from her home; her mother had most of their groceries delivered, and, anyway, Mrs Allsop would never have shopped in such a dimly lit, cellar-smelling place, its windows hung with conflicting advertisements for cigarettes and tea, its shelves crowded promiscuously with faded tins, china souvenirs, regiments of sweet jars. A naked fat ham in orange breadcrumbs jostled for space on the counter with packets of parsley sauce and marked-down broken biscuits. Repulsion at the ham's sickly flesh smell fuelled Jane's impossible swift acts. She chose the cool bottles by feel in the dark little off-licence nook beyond a curtain of plastic strips, because she could hardly see in there; her eyes were dazzled from the light outside. Her heart thudded as violently as an engine stalling, but her hands were sure. The boys paid for the sliced bread and tomatoes and tin of tuna they picked up, thanking the shopkeeper loftily as they left. Jane sat in the car again between them, her trophies chinking on her knee.

— Isn't she good? Paddy said when they'd driven on and he'd excavated in the haversack, finding dusty Mateus rosé and Johnnie Walker and several bottles of barley wine.

— She's a natural, Daniel said.

— Now she belongs to us, Paddy said. — We've got the dirt on her.

Jane sought in the recesses of her consciousness the remorse that she knew ought to be lying in wait – that poor honest shopkeeper, struggling to make a living! But it was as if all recesses had flattened out for the moment, into a balmy infinite present amid the sunshine and the gusts and swirls of wind as the MGC swerved around bends. Her consciousness was filled to the brim with her contact – astonishing because she was so virgin in contacts – with the boys' warm bodies, lapping against her; she didn't even much mind Nigel's chin resting showily on her shoulder, when he leaned over from his perch in the back. It had never occurred to her until now that the masculine – a suspect realm of deep-voiced otherness, beard growth, fact-authority and bathroom smells – could be so intimately important, in relation to herself; it seemed as improbable as two planets colliding.

Now, below the surface of the moment, she began to wait in secret – patiently, because her self-discoveries were very new – for Daniel's hand to jostle her thigh when he changed gears. She stole long gazes at him from behind the blinding strands of her hair, drinking in whatever it was in his looks that tugged at her so exquisitely. His head was poised on his slight frame in a way that reminded her of the poet's bust (she couldn't remember which poet) on the piano at home, which nobody played; his dark hair fell in floppy curls like the poet's sculpted ones, and his face had the same keen, forward-slanting lines. A fine dimple of skin, puckering beside his mouth when he gave one of his rare quick smiles, was a fatal last touch: Jane thought he was as handsome as a rock star or a film star – only more so, because they flaunted crudely from their posters, whereas Daniel held something back.

Nigel had a bottle opener on his key ring, and they started on the barley wine, after a discussion with Jane over whether she drank alcohol or not. — I don't, she owned up candidly. — But I might start. Daniel, solicitous, said that they mustn't give her too much, just a little sip at a time. They watched her face to see whether she liked the taste and laughed delightedly when it was obvious that she didn't, although she bravely insisted (— I do! I do quite like it!), as entertained as if they were feeding beer to a puppy.

If Nigel's parents' house had been anything like Jane's, she might have felt a pang of recollection when they arrived, but although it was secluded behind trees like hers, and with the same defensive air of privilege, it was modern – all glass rectangles and slats of unpainted reddish wood. Somehow it explained Nigel, Jane thought: his angular unease and his gape, as if he were blinking in reflected light. Daniel braked on the gravel with a flourish, and they got out of the car, straggling in through the front of the house and then out again at the back almost immediately, as if the bright indoors were an optical trick, not absorbent like the gloomy interiors Jane was used to, which were dense with family history. A terrace at the back overlooked a garden landscaped in Japanese style, with artful quartz boulders and ginkgo and Japanese maple trees. The boys seemed unsure for a moment what to do next; Jane knew from observing her mother that it was her role to fill awkward silences.

— What a shame I didn't bring my costume, she remarked conversationally, looking at the pool, which Nigel was supposed to skim of its flotsam of twigs and leaves and dead insects every day, but hadn't.

— What costume, Bo Peep? Nigel said. — This isn't a fancy-dress party.

He'd become waspish at the sight of the awful mess in the house, torn between bravado and responsibility (he thought about *his* mother); toying with the idea of washing dishes, he put it aside for later.

— My swimming costume, Jane explained.

Transplanted out of her familiar world, she seemed to find it easier to be dignified, as if she were moving inside a different skin, sleeker. Perhaps it was partly the barley wine. She was able to penetrate, too, into the others' motives and relations – grown-up insight seemed to come not through gradual accretion but all at once. Daniel had power over the other two, she saw, just as he had power over her, though not through any conscious exertion of

13

his will. They tracked his movements and his moods: if he was at ease, then they could be, too. And yet he wasn't tyrannical, was only either pleasant or absent; if he was abstracted, you felt the curse of your failure to interest him. (Paddy, who picked up a book to read as soon as he sat down on the terrace, didn't care as much as she and Nigel did. Because he was cleverer he was more detached, with reserves of irony.) Now Daniel suggested coffee and sandwiches, as if this were a summer lunch party and not the tail end of an all-nighter. The idea made everyone carefree; they discovered they were starving. Nigel hunted in the fridge for butter. If Jane had been older, she might have taken the opportunity to parade her femininity in the kitchen, but it didn't occur to her. Daniel and Nigel made tuna-and-salad-cream sandwiches; she waited with an air of calm entitlement for hers to be brought to her.

While they ate, they catechised her on her opinions, and were delighted to find that she believed in God and expected to vote Conservative when she was twenty-one. (— Not just because my parents do, she insisted. — I shall read the newspapers and make up my own mind.) They were sitting on the terrace in Nigel's mother's striking wicker chairs; Jane's was a shallow cone set in a cast-iron frame. Daniel was cross-legged on the terrace beside her. She said that it was only fair for everyone to do a day's hard work, and that people who criticised England all the time should try going to live somewhere else, and that she hated cruelty to animals. All the time she was talking, Daniel was doing something to her feet,

14

which dangled from the rim of the wicker cone: tickling them with a grass seed head, pulling the grass backwards and forwards between her toes where they were calloused from the thong on her flip-flops. Jane was suffused with a sensation that was mingled ecstasy and shame: shame because she hated her feet, prosaic flat slabs that took an extra-wide fitting. Daniel's feet (he had been barefoot even when he was driving and in the shop – the shop-keeper had stared) were brown and finely complex, high-arched with wire-taut tendons, curling dark hairs tufting each toe.

— D'you think we're layabouts and social parasites? Paddy asked her.

— I thought that perhaps you were students, she said shyly. — I sort of know the type, because my brother's trying for Oxford.

Daniel said that he'd rather not talk about Oxford. — His career there hangs in the balance between brilliance and disaster, Paddy explained on his behalf. (Daniel's senior tutor had warned that after certain brushes with the drug squad he might not be allowed to sit his finals.) — And he doesn't know whether he cares.

— I think we should swim, Daniel suggested. — It's just too fucking hot.

Jane blushed: his word was so forbidden that she hardly knew how she knew it – the girls never used it at school. It was an entrance, glowering with darkness, into the cave of things unknown to her.

— But I haven't got a costume, she said.

— Bo Peep's lost her sheep, Nigel mocked.

15

— Swim nude, Daniel suggested. — No one can see —
except us, and we like you.

She looked around at them all to see if they were joking,
then drew her breath in testingly as you did on the brink
of plunging into water. Inspired (and she had been sipping
barley wine again, with her sandwich), just then she was
capable of anything. Tipping herself out of the cone chair,
she took hold of the hem of her dress, to pull it up over
her head while the boys watched. (It was as easy as playing
with Robin in the old days, she thought, in the garden
with the paddling pool.) She was aware uninhibitedly of
her young body beneath the dress, in its knickers and bra
(she would keep those on, perhaps). But at that very
moment another girl appeared from inside the house,
astonishing them all: she came through the sliding doors,
carrying a glass of fizzing drink ceremoniously, stirring
the ice cubes and sucking at it through a plastic bendy
straw. Slender and disdainful, with a long narrow nose and
slightly squinting eyes, she was wrapped in a sarong. Her
chestnut-dark hair fell well below her waist in symmetrical
waves, as if it had been tied in plaits and then undone.

— She can borrow my old swimsuit if she wants, the
girl said, with an air of unmasking male proceedings
beneath her dignity.

Nigel had leaped out of his chair, a suspended wicker
basket, which went swinging wildly. — Fiona! When did
you get here? How did you get in? What on earth are
you drinking?

— Vodka, Fiona said. — And I got in while you were
out, because you actually failed to lock anything up

behind you, you idiot. I mean, God, Nige, what if I'd been a burglar or something? Then I was fast asleep, until you lot started banging around down here. And this pool's a disgusting swamp – weren't you supposed to do something about it? Hi, Daniel and Paddy. Hi, what's-your-name. My cozzy's in a drawer in the chest in my bedroom, if you want it.

Fiona was Nigel's younger sister, aged eighteen and returned by herself from the South of France on her way to drama school. She chose to sit with her drink under an orange umbrella at the far end of the terrace, as if she were semi-detached from her brother and his friends. But Jane, with her new intuitiveness, guessed that she sat there because it meant that she was in Daniel's sightlines the whole time she was yawning and stretching and pretending to sunbathe, showing off her legs through the slit in her sarong.

Jane borrowed Fiona's swimming costume (which was tight on her) and powered up and down the short pool with her strong crawl, face turning into the water then out to breathe, as she'd been taught, all the accumulated rubbish (leathery wet leaves, sodden drowned butterflies and daddy-long-legs, an empty cigarette pack) bobbing against her breasts and lips and knees as she swam. No one joined her in the pool. Jane had hardly expected them to; she had accepted immediately the justice of her defeat – right at the moment that she'd had all the boys' eyes on her – by the older, prettier, more sophisticated girl. (Still, the word 'woebegone' nudged at her, from a poem she'd read at school.) When she got out, she would ask Paddy to drive her to a bus stop, then to lend her the money for her bus fare home. She would ask for his address, so that she could repay him: out of her pocket money, because she could never tell her parents where she'd been.

Heaving herself out at the side of the pool, she stood streaming water, too shy to ask for a towel. The others were planning a visit to the pub in the nearest village. Jane had never been inside a pub in her life, but she thought there was bound to be a bus stop somewhere in the village.

— Come on, let's go, Fiona said impatiently. There was only half an hour until afternoon closing time.

— We can't all get in the car, Nigel said, worrying.

— We can if we hold on tight. It'll be a scream. Paddy, come on.

Obediently Paddy stood up, stuffing his book into his back pocket. (It was Herman Hesse's *Steppenwolf.*) He went to look for shoes. Fiona was aware suddenly of Jane. — Oh, God, she's still got that costume on. Can't you just put your dress on over the top?

Jane looked down mutely at herself, still dripping.

Daniel hadn't moved from where he was spreadeagled now in a deckchair. He'd been watching Jane's steady stroke in the pool, how she submitted to the rhythm of it and forgot herself, forgot to wonder whether they were looking at her or not. He had felt, while he watched, that he was seeing deeply into her raw sensibility: fatalistic, acutely responsive, open to anything. He was aware all the time, of course, of Fiona's manoeuvring to make him notice her – there was a bit of past history between them, which he was wary of reviving, not wanting her to get it into her head that she had any rights of possession over him. Anyway, her blasé, bossy voice was grating on him this afternoon. Her displays of sophistication seemed childish, and he was unmoved by the skinny brown stomach flashing at him so insistently from above the sarong.

— You go ahead, he said. — Jane has to change. I'll wait and walk down with her. We'll catch up.

Fiona couldn't hide the sour disappointment in her face, but she had staked too much, too noisily, on her desperate need for the pub to back down now. Jane looked anxiously from one to the other. — I don't mind, she said. — You don't have to wait for me.

— What are you up to, Daniel? Fiona laughed ungraciously.

Daniel kept his eyes closed against the sun while the others quarrelled, getting ready; Jane went inside to change. When he heard the car receding on the road, he followed her in, confused at first in the interior patchwork of light and shadows, after the glare outdoors. He stood listening at the bottom of the open-tread staircase, his breath barely stirring the bright dust motes in their circling. The house was as perfectly quiet as if it were empty, yet he was aware of the girl standing somewhere upstairs, equally still, listening for him. The moment seemed eloquent, as he put his foot on the bottom step and started up, breaking into the peace.

He found Jane in Fiona's room, where she'd left her dress; she was still in the wet costume, although she'd pulled down the blind out of modesty, so that he saw her waiting in a pink half-light. (She'd been afraid, suddenly, to be naked, in case he came looking for her.) His mouth when he kissed her (her first-ever kiss) seemed scalding, because her mouth was cold from the water and from fear. She was cold and clammy all over. When Daniel tried to peel off the sodden swimming costume it knotted itself around her in a rubbery clinging rope and she had to help, rolling it and dragging at it. They left it where it lay when she kicked it off, and its wetness soaked into Fiona's red rug.

Fiona found the wet patch on her rug later and guessed immediately (she had intuitions, too) the story behind it; she thought for one outraged moment that they'd actually done it on her bed. But her bed was intact – thank God for that, at least. Daniel must have taken Jane into the spare room, where he and Paddy were staying. By now it was late afternoon, and Jane was in a phone box in the village, ringing home. (Nigel didn't want them using the phone at the house, in case his parents complained about the bill.) Daniel waited for her, not interested in her difficulties over what to say. He was smoking, leaning back against the phone box, head tilted to look up at the sky, which was still immaculately blue, just beginning to pale. Even while Jane spoke to her mother in the ordinary words that seemed to flow convincingly, as if from her old self, her new self pressed her free palm on the rectangle of thick glass against which, on the other side, Daniel in his blue shirt was also miraculously pressed, oblivious of her touch. (And she knew now the long brown nakedness of his back under the shirt, with its ripple of vertebrae.) Forever afterwards, the smell inside one of those old red phone boxes – dank and mushroomy and faintly urinous – could turn Jane's heart over in erotic excitement.

Her mother's mild voice was in her ear, incurious: they had begun to wonder where she was. – I told Daddy you'd probably gone off to play ping-pong somewhere.

– I'm at Alison's, Jane said. – Alison Lefanu. You remember, from Junior Orchestra? French horn. Can I stay the night? It doesn't matter about toothbrush and pyjamas. Her mum says I can borrow them.

Mrs Allsop, blessedly vague, sent her love to Mrs Lefanu. – The Lefanus live out at Headley, don't they? You didn't walk all that way?

– I was on my way down to the village, and they drove past. I just got in.

Jane was thinking, Will I ever see my home again? It seemed unlikely.

– Don't be a nuisance, her mother said. – Eat whatever they put in front of you, even if it's cauliflower.

Now they all sat talking on the terrace in an evening light as thick as syrup; clouds of insects swarmed above the Japanese water features, swallows slipped close along the earth, a blackbird sang. They were drinking

Jane's shoplifted wine and her whisky; then the boys started messing around with a needle and little glass vials of methedrine, which Paddy fetched from his room. — Don't look, it's not for nice girls, Daniel said to Jane, and so, obediently, she closed her eyes. The boys' huddle over this ceremony – so intimate, taken so seriously – frightened Fiona and made her even more furious than the wet patch on her rug. She went inside and crashed around the house, effecting a transformation: washing dishes, scrubbing the stove and the kitchen floor, throwing the windows wide open, emptying ashtrays with a clang of the dustbin lid. She shook out the mats from the sitting room, cracking them like whips over the boys' heads on the terrace. Gradually, as she worked, the resentment slipped out of her and her mood changed. She began to enjoy her own strength and to feel serenely indifferent to the others. If her brother's friends wanted to get doped up, why should she care? She started to think about drama school. Later, she warmed up some tinned soup, and brought out cheese and crackers for them all. By this time it was dark and the only light came from the lamps she'd turned on inside.

Daniel was trying to explain the idea of the soul as it was understood in the Hindu Vedanta. His words were punctuated by the clonk of the bamboo shishi-odoshi in the garden, which filled up with water then tipped and emptied, falling back against its rock. What he wanted to describe was how the soul's origins were in wholeness and light, but on its entry into the world it took on the filth of violence and corruption. The soul trapped in the individual forgot its home and despaired; but despair was only another illusion to be stripped away. He wanted to say that revolution was a kind of cleansing that conferred its own immortality in a perpetual present. Art had to be revolutionary or it would die in time. He believed as he spoke that he was brilliantly eloquent, but in truth he was rambling incoherently.

Paddy, getting the gist of it, quoted poetry in an ironic voice: — 'Heard melodies are sweet, but those unheard are sweeter.'

— Signor Keats, I do believe, Nigel said.

— Oh, that's the poet, Jane said. — We have his bust at home, on the piano.

Cross-legged on a cushion at Daniel's feet, she was leaning lightly against him, as if she could ground the tension quivering in his right foot, which was balanced across his left knee. His intelligence seemed as ceaseless as an engine working. She felt exceptionally attuned to the boys' voices rising through earnestness to mockery and back again, although she hardly heard their words, only what ran underneath: a current of strain, a jostling of contest and display. She saw how Nigel tried to match the other two and failed, and how he suffered, yearning for Daniel's approval. Meanwhile her own new knowledge filled her up, not in the form of thoughts but as sensations, overwhelming. Her experience in the strange bed that afternoon hadn't been joyous: there'd been some swooning, obliterating pleasure in the preliminaries, but then too much anxiety in the clumsy arrangements which she had known (from her biology lessons) would follow. Remembering it all now, though, she was sick with desire and longed for the time to come when Daniel would touch her again.

When they did go to bed, however, Daniel was suddenly exhausted; stoop-backed, he crawled between the sheets in his underpants, turning away from Jane, towards the window. — Watch over me, was the last thing he mumbled.

And so she kept vigil faithfully for hours in the quiet of the night, presiding over the mystery of her changed life, adjusting her body against the peremptory curve of his turned back and legs in the narrow single bed. But at last she couldn't help it – she fell asleep herself. And when she awoke in the morning Daniel was gone. After a while, when he didn't come back, she put on her underclothes and her dress, and set off around the house in search of him. Downstairs, she smelled Paddy's sweat and saw the tousled mess of his hair poking from the top of a sleeping bag on the sofa in the lounge. Nigel was making a racket outside with the sliding door of the garage, in search of the net for the swimming pool. Jane climbed upstairs again. Nigel's parents' bedroom was at the front of the house, opening off the landing ahead of her; the door was ajar, and Jane stepped soundlessly inside.

It was a beautiful room, like nothing she'd ever seen before, with a pale wood floor and plain white walls, creamy sheepskin rugs. Fresh sunlight, pouring through windows all along its length, was reflected in the mirrored doors of the built-in wardrobes; the curtains, in some kind of rough white translucent linen, were cut too long for the windows, and the cloth fell in heaps on the floor. A huge bed seemed to be all white sheets and no blankets. (Jane had never seen a duvet before.) In the bed, with the duvet kicked to their feet, Daniel and Fiona lay naked and asleep, facing away from each other, their slim tanned legs tangled together. Jane, who had done the Greeks in history, thought that they looked like young warriors in a classical scene, fallen in the place where they had been wrestling. She withdrew from the room without waking them, as quietly as she had come in.

Nigel, rather the worse for wear, in his pyjama bottoms, was smoking and skimming the pool, dumping the rubbish in a soaking heap beside him. He watched when Jane came to stand at the pool's brink; she stared in with dry, hot eyes.

— So now you know, he said.

But she repudiated his offer of companionship in her unrequited love. Her experience was not like anyone else's. She asked only if he would drive her back, and he said he'd get the car out as soon as he'd finished with the pool.

— I'd like to go now, she said crisply, sounding like her mother. — If you don't mind.

On the way they hardly spoke, except when Nigel asked for directions as they drew near her home. Jane forgot, in her absorption, to notice the way they'd come, so that she never afterwards knew where Nigel's house was. And she never saw it again, or any of the boys (Fiona once, perhaps, at a party).

He dropped her off at the bottom of the drive. It was still quite early in the morning – only nine o'clock. Jane stared around her as if she'd never seen the place before, as if it were more mysterious than anywhere she'd been – the scuffed dirt at the edge of the road, the old mossy gateposts, blackbirds flitting in the dead leaves at the bottom of the hedge, the hard lime-yellow fruits in the hedge apple tree, her own footprints from the day before intact in the dust, the Jokari paddle left where she had dropped it.

Her mother didn't seem surprised to see her so early.
— Did you have a nice time, dear?
Jane said that she'd had fun. But that afternoon she suffered with pain in her stomach and bloating (— What exactly did you eat at the Lefanus'?). And the next day her period came rather copiously and early – which ought to have been a relief but wasn't, because it hadn't occurred to her until then (despite the biology lessons) that she could be pregnant. The weather changed, too. So it was all right for her to curl up under her eider-down, hugging a hot-water bottle to her stomach, reading her Chalet School books and looking up from time to time at the rain running down the window. Her mother brought her tea with two sugars, and aspirin.

Jane never told anyone what had happened to her (not even, years later, the boyfriend who became her husband, and who might have wondered). And in a way she never assimilated the experience, though she didn't forget it, either. As an adult, she took on board all the usual Tory disapproval towards drugs and juvenile delinquency and underage sex, and never saw any implications for her own case. She was fearful for her own daughters, as normal mothers were, without connecting her fears to anything that had happened to her. Her early initiation stayed in a sealed compartment in her thoughts and seemed to have no effects, no consequences.

Jane and her husband divorced in their mid-fifties, and her friends advised her to have counselling. The counsellor was a nice, intelligent woman. (Actually, she couldn't help feeling exasperated by Jane and her heavy, patient sorrows: her expensive clothes, her lack of imagination, the silk scarf thrown girlishly over one shoulder. Of course, she was much too professional to let this show.) Jane confessed that she had always felt as if she were on the wrong side of a barrier, cutting her off from the real life she was meant to be living.

— What's it like, then, real life on the other side?

Haltingly, Jane described a summer day beside a swimming pool. A long sunlit room with white walls and a white bed. A breeze is blowing; long white curtains are dragged sluggishly backwards and forwards on a pale wood floor. (These women's fantasies, the counsellor thought, have more to do with interior decor than with repressed desires.) Then Jane got into her stride, and the narrative became more interesting. — A boy and a girl, she said, — are naked, asleep in the bed. I am curled on a rug on the floor beside them. The boy turns over in his sleep, flings out his arm, and his hand dangles to the floor. I think he's seeking out the cool, down there under the bed. I move carefully on my rug, so as not to wake him. I move so that his hand is touching me.

That's more like it, the counsellor thought. That's something.

As for Daniel, well, he trained as a lawyer after he'd finished his literature degree. He got out of the drink and the drugs not long after university. (Paddy never did; he died.) Daniel lives in Geneva now, with his second wife, whom he loves very much, and occasionally, when he's bored with his respectable Swiss friends and wants to shock them, he tells stories about his wild youth. He is in international human-rights law; he's a force for good. He's a good husband and father, too (more dedi-cated, because of the wildness in his past). Of course, he's ambitious and likes power.

He can just about remember Nigel, and Nigel's parents' house that summer, and Fiona (they were together off and on for a few months afterwards). But he has no memory at all of Jane. Even if by some miracle he ever met her, and she recognised him and told him the whole story (which she would never do), it wouldn't bring anything back. It isn't only that the drink and the drugs made him forget. He's had too much happiness in his life since, too much experience; he's lost that fine-tuning that could hold on to the smell of the ham in the off-licence, the wetness of the swimming costume, the girl's cold skin and her naivety, her extraordinary offer of herself without reserve, the curtains sweeping the floor in the morning light. It's all just gone.

The Stain

T he old man's daughter made enquiries in the village, looking for someone to go there every weekday and keep an eye on him, to clean the place and cook something for his lunch and tea. He wasn't incapacitated, but he wasn't used to looking after himself. Marina needed the money. So every morning, after she dropped Liam off at school, she made her way up through the churchyard and across the park to the square stone house on the corner where the old man lived. Rooks squawked, scattered out of the beech trees by the wind; unkempt grass blew around the molehills; swallows were dark scratches on the light. Marina was tall and athletic-looking, in black leggings and trainers and a pink Puffa jacket, with a freckled face and a ponytail of tangled curling auburn hair. She walked with a long stride, swinging her shopping bag, bent forward as if she were oblivious or shy, although she was well known in the village. She'd had plenty of little jobs doing house-work, and had worked in the dry-cleaner's before she was married. Reliable and thoughtful, an oddball who kept herself apart from the other mothers, she was just the right choice for handling a difficult old man.

She told him that she had been looking at this house all her life – she'd passed it every day when she was a child herself, walking to school – but she'd never been inside before. She didn't volunteer this right away; she waited first to see whether he wanted her to talk. Her husband Gary had warned her that the old man and his daughter would be used to having black servants waiting on them hand and foot, but it wasn't really like that. Wendy had left South Africa and come to live in England before Marina was even born, and she said that she never wanted to go back – there was so much violence there now. And the old man didn't seem to be any kind of slave-driver. He liked to sit and watch Marina work sometimes, but he always asked her courteously first whether she minded.

— So what d'you think of the house, now you're inside it? he asked.

— You've got a nice lot of space, she said, sitting back on her haunches, wiping her hot face on her arm. She was scouring the linoleum on the kitchen floor, on her hands and knees with a scrubbing brush and a bucket, because of the stubborn greasy dirt. She told him that you could fit her whole house in his drawing room. When she was a child, this house from the outside, with its tall facade and many blind-looking windows, had seemed to stand for all the grandeur and beauty she could imagine. In reality, inside it was dingy and half furnished and needed a coat of paint. The kitchen and the bathrooms hadn't been altered in thirty years; in the kitchen she had to manage with a single stainless-steel sink and no dishwasher. The previous owners had left some furniture in the upstairs rooms, but the upholstery was worn and grubby; the old man hadn't brought much from South Africa. They had plenty of money: Wendy's own place was as luxurious inside as pictures in a magazine. It was the old man's choice, his obstinacy, to live in the house without renovating it.

He missed the sun, sitting with a blanket over his knees even in warm weather. Although he was eighty-nine, he didn't look that old. He was thickset with broad shoulders, his white hair sprouting up stiffly, his small eyes, lost under baggy eyelids, set far back above his flattened cheekbones. His face was expressive and ravaged, like an actor's. Marina imagined how hard it was for a man who must once have been so vigorous to accept this diminished life, using a cane to get around, with no one to command except her. He'd had to give up driving because of his glaucoma; anyway, he had no friends to visit in this country, apart from his daughter. Because he talked about the vines he'd tended in South Africa, and because he was so deeply tanned, his skin like tough yellow leather, Marina thought he must have been a farmer and spent his days outdoors.

The vacuum cleaner died on Marina one morning while she was doing the stairs, and he told her to bring it to where he was sitting, in the room he called the office, poring over bank statements and bills. (He had business interests, he told her, though he wasn't a businessman.) He took the thing to pieces with a screwdriver on top of the desk, painstakingly, with trembling fingers, peering at it through his magnifying glass. When he was concentrating, he stuck out the tip of his tongue at one corner of his mouth, just as Liam did. He got the vacuum going again and that cheered him up. Marina noticed that at lunch that day he ate more hungrily. He said that he liked meat, meat more than anything, and he complimented her gravy (everybody liked her gravy), but usually he managed only a few mouthfuls, pushing whatever vegetables she'd cooked for him to one side of the plate. She had to tuck a napkin under his chin, to keep him from dropping food on his shirtfront.

The next day she brought an Airfix model in her shopping bag, a Spitfire that someone had given Liam for Christmas; it was too difficult for Liam, and she wondered if the old man would enjoy putting it together. She worried that she was overstepping the mark, insulting him with a child's toy, but he seemed pleased; he told her that he'd had a pilot's licence for years, flying small planes. His hands weren't steady enough, though, to control the tiny pieces of the model – you needed tweezers to put the pilot and the propellers in place, and the glue got everywhere, the pieces stuck to his fingers. Marina had to help him paint it and put the stickers on, according to the instructions. He was discouraged and disappointed in himself; he blamed his eyes.

— You could write your memoirs, she suggested. — That's what my grandpa did, because he was in the war. He dictated them into a recorder, and my auntie typed them up. You could pay someone to do it.

The old man laughed sourly, tapping his forehead. — Better not. Better to keep it all in here where it's safe.

She got him to talk about the weather in South Africa, the landscape and the wild animals. He said that the fruit and vegetables over here tasted of nothing, so she picked peas and broad beans from his own vegetable patch, which Wendy tended, and got him to shell them for her, sitting in his garden, saucepan on his lap, colander at his side for the empty pods. If you asked him in the right way, as though you needed his help, then he didn't mind being put to work. When he'd shelled them himself, he would sometimes eat them with his lunch.

She saw that he was depressed because he was bored. She could tell as soon as she arrived in the morning if he was in a mood. He sulked; he pretended not to hear her come in the back door, calling out to him; he knocked things over deliberately; he snarled into the phone. (He was always on the telephone, fussing over his investments.) When he was pleased with himself, he was emotional, jovial. He snatched Marina's hand and squeezed it, said that she was like another daughter to him. There were real tears in his eyes. He wanted to know all about Gary and Liam and her parents and her childhood. He liked to hear the story of her walking past his house when she was a girl. — I wish I'd lived here then, he said. — I'd have invited you inside. You could have played in the garden.

But once he pushed her hand away in irritation when she brought him a cup of hot coffee, so that it spilled all down her front, and then he was in an agony of contrition – he tried to get down on his knees to ask forgiveness. — Don't be so silly, Marina said calmly. — I'm not scalded. And it's only an old apron.

— Can I buy you a new washing machine? he said. — I mean for your own home. To make up for it. I'm a horrible old man.

She laughed. — Listen to you. What are you on about? I've got a perfectly good washing machine.

Wendy called at the house most days, in her four-by-four with tinted windows and the two dogs in the back – to drop off her father's shopping, or to work in his garden, or take him to his medical appointments (he had prostate problems and diabetes). She wasn't known for her tact; she was always managing to upset the women who worked for her in her fancy gift shop (which was only a hobby – her divorce had left her with more than enough money). But Marina didn't take offence when Wendy tried ordering her around, finding fault. Wendy was a dumpy little woman, nervous and punctilious, with the same wide-apart eyes and flattened cheekbones as the old man, her hair dyed black and cut in a shape like a pixie's cap. Apparently she had a wardrobe full of beautiful clothes that she couldn't get into any more. You could hardly hear her South African accent, though you could cut her father's with a knife.

After all those years apart, father and daughter were almost strangers to each other; Wendy was embarrassed if he had to lean on her for support when they went out together, for drinks or to a concert in the village. He was forceful and charming, and made a point of winning over Wendy's friends, but she was awkward in his company. She knew how to show affection only to her dogs. She'd wanted her father to come over, but now that she'd got him here she didn't know what to do with him. People said that there was a brother still in South Africa, but the family had lost touch with him; he'd had mental-health problems, or he'd spent time in prison for cheating pensioners out of their money.

Marina was settling in at the big house. When she went up to dust the bedrooms on the second floor, which were never used, she liked to stand dreaming, looking down from the windows on her old life in the street below. She persuaded the old man to come to church with her on Sundays. And she took Liam to play in the garden after school, thinking that it would be good for the old man. He'd hardly known his grandchildren, Wendy's three sons, when they were small, and they didn't seem eager to make contact with him now. One was an architect and one was in banking; Anthony, the youngest, still lived at home, and was supposed to be setting up some sort of business on the Internet. Glancing out from the kitchen, where she was fixing something that the old man could heat up for his tea later, Marina saw his white head and Liam's round fair head bent intently over something or other that Liam had dug up out of the earth – a snail shell or a broken bit of china. The flame of her love for her child lapped for that moment around the lonely old man, too: the baggy, age-spotted hands cupping the child's tiny, unspoiled, tender ones.

Wendy came into the kitchen with a basket full of courgettes and lettuce, wanting to wash her hands in the sink, clicking her tongue impatiently when she saw it was full of peelings. Holding her hands under the running water, she stared out of the window at her father playing with Liam. — He was never like that with us, she said, not as if she were complaining, just passing on information. Sometimes when she'd been working in the garden her usual stiffness unwound. — He's growing garrulous in his old age. Child-friendly. Religious. What a turn-up.

— You grew up on a farm, didn't you?

— Is that what he told you?

— He talked about growing things.

— There was a farm in the Cape. It was my grandparents', but we always kept it up. And Dad made a go of it again after he retired. Just something to keep him busy.

Mostly Wendy kept herself carefully closed off from Marina behind a preoccupied, worldly surface, always hurrying somewhere, flashing her car keys about like an insignia. In the back of the four-by-four, along with the dogs, there were boxes full of the retro stuff she sold for so much money in her shop: enamel watering cans artfully rusted, worn old trowels tied up with hairy twine,

38

bits of slate to use as plant labels, rickety iron garden chairs, carbolic soap. These were for people who played at gardening, Marina thought. But Wendy herself was an expert, gifted gardener. As well as growing vegetables in her father's garden, she was clearing the little paths edged with lavender around an old sundial, and replanting the herbaceous border in front of the yew hedge with delphinium, verbascum and phlox.

In church, Marina only half listened to the words of the service; she went into a kind of trance. She sometimes thought she might fall asleep while she had her head in her hands and was meant to be praying. The important thing was her immersion in the subdued light and the pocket of damp, different air inside the church walls. Afterwards, she and Liam walked the old man back across the park; he leaned on her, stumbling on the tussocky grass, making her feel his dead weight. His force hadn't drained away altogether, but it was uncoordinated, outside his control. He wore dark glasses in the sunshine to protect his eyes. At the house, she would pour him a brandy and settle him to wait for Wendy, who came to fetch him for Sunday lunch. He didn't want the television on – he said he couldn't see it, didn't care for it anyway.

— Watch out for him, Gary said. — Old men get some funny ideas.

But nothing ever happened that was wrong. He kissed her on the cheek with his wet mouth every day when she arrived and when she left; if he got the chance he tried to put his arm around her shoulders or her waist. Once or twice he touched her legs, not lewdly, but she reproached him and he was abashed; he retreated into gloom, wouldn't speak for hours. Marina didn't tell Gary about any of this. She thought how hard it must be, at the end of your life, to be deprived forever of physical contact. Her own body felt luxuriantly wrapped in touching – Gary's and Liam's. She hardly knew where her body stopped and her little boy's started. Couldn't she spare the old man a little out of her surplus?

— I'm sorry for him, she said to Gary. — And the money's useful.

Gary worked for his brother, who laid patios and garden paths, but there wasn't much business; people were cutting back in the recession. Marina didn't tell him, either, that the old man put extra money in the envelope he gave her every week, crushing it clumsily into her pocket or into the bib of her apron while she was rolling out plain scones on the kitchen table. Every week, once she'd washed and dried her hands and counted the money, she took out the extra and gave it firmly back to him, so that there could be no mistake. She knew where to draw the line.

— Please take it, he said, pushing it at her. — There's plenty more where that came from. Make me happy by taking it. What do I want with it now, at my age, in this condition? I want to give it to your family.

— These are just dreams, she said. — They're nonsense. You don't know us.

40

— You're good people, I know you are. I watch you. I want to help your husband out, let him start up a little business of his own. I want to set up a trust fund, so that your boy can go to a decent school.

— To give something like that to someone, you have to be a relative. Or you have to have known them all your life, through thick and thin. This story you've dreamed up about us isn't real. You haven't even met my husband.

— It's you who doesn't know about the real world, he said impatiently. — Money changes things, if you've got it. You can change anything.

— I don't want change, then.

— I don't believe you.

Sometimes after church he persuaded her to have a drop of brandy with him in the drawing room while he waited for Wendy. It was sweet, and not harsh as she'd expected; she rarely drank alcohol, so it went straight to her head. Liam would be playing in the garden. Because of the brandy, when she saw him from the window she seemed to be looking down on him from a great distance, at his bare knees and bent head as he crouched, stroking the neighbours' tabby. She could hear the coaxing, chirruping noises he was making. The drawing room ran right through the house – it had sash windows at front and back. She loved the way the light sprang across from one wall to the other, as if in a conversation.

The old man told her that all his life he'd thought only about his career and not enough about his family; he'd forgotten the religion he'd believed in when he was a boy. He said that after his wife died he'd gone off the rails – he'd been with all kinds of women, he'd paid for prostitutes. Would God forgive him? Marina stopped him. She said that it wasn't right for her to know those things if his own daughter didn't.

— Could I tell her? he barked, in an outbreak of rough contempt.

All the time Marina kept him safely at arm's length, putting him off gently, smiling, laughing. But he told her nonetheless that she was a beautiful and graceful young woman. (Those weren't words that Gary ever would have used.) She was ashamed of feeling secretly gratified. She said that he had to stop talking such rubbish. He told her about his travels all over Africa. He'd been to Singapore and Cairo and Australia and California. Marina knew that she was unsophisticated, that her life must seem tame and timid to him. Sometimes it seemed timid to her; she chafed against its limits. The old man held something back, some knowledge or intimation, which made her life seem shallow by comparison – even if he was cantankerous and shaky on his legs, with his cavernous stale mouth and brown teeth.

Then he wanted to give her the house. The story went round the village as a half-secret. Ten bedrooms, Queen Anne, Grade II-listed; it needed work, but had to be worth a million at least, even in the current market. Properties at the top of the ladder hadn't lost much. The women in the shop looked at Wendy to see how she was taking it: she'd brought her father all the way over here

to be with her, and now he was giving away her inheritance to the cleaning lady. (Though there was probably
plenty more, apart from the house. He'd been putting
money into a British bank account for years.)

Marina knew what everyone was thinking. Of course
she couldn't take the house. What would they do, in any
case – her and Gary and Liam – with all those rooms?
The maintenance of those old places cost a fortune in
itself; it would fall down around their ears. It was the
old man's fantasy – she never seriously considered it. He
begged her to accept, and she refused. Then he told
Wendy that he was leaving it to Marina anyway. There
was a big confrontation; Wendy accused the pair of them
of scheming behind her back. Marina, in tears, gave in
her notice.

That evening, Wendy telephoned to apologise. — I
shouldn't have lost my temper, she said. — We're both
distraught at having upset you. I'd be so grateful if you'd
give us another try. It would be difficult for us to find
anyone else. My father's not an easy man, and he's grown
very fond of you.

— But you'll always think I'm after his money, Marina
said.

Wendy recoiled at her bluntness, she could hear. (She
had blenched once when Marina brought an armful of
dirty sheets into the kitchen after the old man had had
an accident in his bed.)— I'm sure it was all his idea, she
offered with chilly neutrality. — I know what my father's
like, once he fixes on something.

— I'll go back if he stops trying to give me stuff.

— He says he's sorry. It won't happen again.

So Marina resumed making her way each morning, after she'd dropped Liam off at school, under the soughing, agitated trees in the churchyard and across the park – head down as usual, her long scissoring stride like a wading bird's – to spend all day alone with the old man. Wendy offered her a rise, and she accepted it; Gary had always said that she ought to be paid better for the work she did, more like a full-time carer than a cleaner. (And, after all that, the extra was only deducted from her working tax credit.)

For a while, after their row, the old man treated Marina as if she were made of glass, putting on a meek, modestly enquiring voice that wasn't really his, asking for a gin and tonic before his lunch but 'only if she had time'. This was nonsense and they both knew it, were relieved when he fell back into his usual peremptory intimacy. At least he'd stopped giving her presents. Yet, in some magical way, Marina did now succumb to the idea that the old house was hers – not forever but for the moment. She was getting to know it now that she had gone into every corner of it, scouring out the gritty dust and cobwebs and curled-up balls of dead woodlice, bleaching and disinfecting. She had even grown not to mind the faded furniture and the empty rooms, the staring rectangles on the wallpaper, where the previous owners had taken down their paintings. She cut flowers in the garden and arranged them in vases that she found in a cupboard under the stairs.

She put out a linen napkin in a silver ring for the old man's lunch.

— Won't you sit with me? he asked her humbly.

The food that Wendy brought him was too rich, cooked in olive oil or with cream sauces; he couldn't always keep it down. Marina made plain food, and she cut the meat into little pieces for him, easy to chew and swallow. He got angry with his broken body, how it betrayed him. She rested her hand consolingly on his shoulder while he ate. She knew that she was a good nurse; her hands were good. She had looked after her own father in his last illness.

For the old man's ninetieth birthday party, Wendy built a barbecue out of bricks, in a little paved area by one corner of the wall at the end of the garden. She told Marina that when she was a child she and her brother had spent every summer on their farm in the Western Cape, cooking most of their food outdoors on a braai or in a metal potjie, which sat over the fire. The old man was pleased with the idea of a party; it gave him something to look forward to. On the telephone, he ordered crates of his favourite Groot Constantia wine.

His birthday was at the end of September and the sky was cloudless. Guests – mostly friends of Wendy's – came strolling across the grass from where they had parked beside the church. The vicar came, with the next-door neighbours, and Anthony and another of Wendy's sons, who brought his wife. Anthony and his brother took charge of grilling the meat, entering into the role with a lot of teasing banter, deferring to their grandfather's expertise. They were good-looking young men, casually but expensively dressed, aware of conferring the favour of their youth on the elderly party. Marina had spoken to Anthony once or twice when he came to the house with Wendy; she'd never met the other one before. The old man had insisted that she bring Gary and Liam, though Gary was reluctant, sure he'd have nothing to say to these kinds of people. She had persuaded him to come for just an hour. At least he had Liam to look after; his responsibility for his son gave him something to do in a crowd and made him more confident.

The guests gathered closer together, as the light went, around the barbecue's radiant heat. Gary enjoyed himself after all. The old man made a fuss of him, filling up his glass; he wasn't used to drinking wine and it helped him talk more easily, mostly about the local fishing. As if she were in a conspiracy with the old man, Marina noticed how cleverly he charmed her husband – while Liam, the only child at the party, ran in the dusk around the winding garden paths, lost in his own world. When Marina went into the kitchen to wash up, Wendy followed her, protesting theatrically that she could take it all home to put in her dishwasher. Wendy had been drinking, too; in company her manner was jokey, almost flirtatious. She must have been pleased at having her handsome sons on display. She thanked Marina emotionally for every-thing she'd done for the old man, said she thought her dad was having a great day. Drying up the plates and cutlery and putting them away, Marina was relieved that the tension between her and Wendy seemed to be resolved; she covered the leftover food with cling film, restored order in the quiet kitchen. Gary took Liam home to put him to bed; she said she'd follow them soon. Voices floated subduedly through the open window. She knew the pattern of her movements in that kitchen by heart – her hand found its way in the shadows to each cupboard door or drawer. Tightening the taps, she wrung out the dishcloth and hung it across the drainer.

She would have liked to slip away invisibly, but the old man called her over as she stepped out of the back door. (They never used the grand front door, which opened onto the street.) She was surprised that he could even see her through his dark glasses, from the far end of the garden; he had seemed sunk in sleep, hunched silent in his chair with a shawl over his shoulders as the others talked. Only his family were left around the barbecue. Wendy's daughter-in-law, Jasmine, was yawning and shivering in her skimpy dress. Half standing up, the old man fumbled for Marina's hand and kissed it.

— Where have you been hiding away from me?

Everyone laughed. His words were slurring. She thought he'd had enough of the party and was probably ready for bed. — Have you met Marina, Jasmine? She's my treasure.

Wendy chimed in. — We are very lucky to have Marina.

The old man wanted belatedly to make a speech. — I've been so fortunate to be surrounded with love in my old age, in a strange country where I didn't look for it. Marina doesn't know her own goodness. People like her and her family, they hold it all together for the rest of us, in their spirit. Some of us have had lives with every advantage, but we don't deserve to kiss the hem of her garment.

Marina was embarrassed, and jarred by some false, sentimental note in his performance, which seemed aimed challengingly at his family. She pulled her hand away quickly. Anthony offered her a lift; he said he wanted an excuse to try out his brother's Audi, but she insisted that she preferred to walk – it would take her only ten minutes. It was a relief to be out on the street alone. The high heels she'd worn for the party clicked and scraped too assertively on the pavement, so she bent and eased them off, then walked barefoot, carrying her shoes with the straps looped over her finger. She should have brought her trainers to change into. There was no one around, but a car came up behind her as she turned into the road off the high street which led to the little estate of ex-council houses where she lived. There was no pavement here, so she stood back for the car to pass. Instead, it drew up alongside her, sleek and low-slung, engine thrumming fluently. Anthony leaned across to push open the passenger door, his white shirt gleaming in the light from the instrument panel.

— Get in, he said. — I'm driving it back to Mum's. I'll drop you off.

— Really, I like the walk, Marina protested. — Clears my head.

But he wouldn't take no for an answer. When she moved on, he followed at her speed, nosing the car along in stops and starts, revving the engine persuasively. She felt its hot breath on her bare legs. Anthony opened the door again. — Come on. Hop in.

Exasperated, conscious that people must be listening behind all the windows in the street, she got in. Despite the fine night, Anthony had the air conditioning on, and in the sealed, cold atmosphere the smell of the leather upholstery was strong. — Nice motor, isn't it? he said. He dropped his glance briefly from the road, noticing her feet. — You funny thing. You've taken your shoes off.

— Can't walk quick in my heels.

He was amused. — But don't you mind getting your feet dirty?

— Take the left here at the fork. Then it's the first right.

— I know where you live. But we're going the long way round. I want to have a little talk with you.

Marina was furious with herself for having accepted the lift against her better judgement. — Don't be silly, Anthony. I'm tired and I want to get home.

She rattled the handle of the car door, but Anthony seemed to have locked it by pressing something on his side; he put his foot down on the accelerator. They left the last houses of the village behind and were quickly onto the country road, where the car's headlights tunnelled into the darkness under the trees. Marina wasn't frightened – she was too full of outrage, folding her arms tightly around her bag and pressing it to her chest. How dare he carry her off as if she didn't count? They were probably more or less the same age, she and this boy, but she felt herself immeasurably older than he was. She had a child of her own, whereas he still lived like a child

49

in his mother's house; Wendy complained that he left his dirty clothes on the floor for her to pick up. Yet somehow Anthony undermined her with self-doubt – his fresh, plump face unmarked by trouble and his voice so blandly assured.

— Please take me back, she said as calmly as she could, and Anthony assured her that he'd turn around as soon as he had the chance. About a quarter of a mile up the road, he steered the Audi into a lay-by where tourists sometimes parked their cars to walk the forest trails. Marina struggled again with the door.

— Let me out here, she insisted. — I want to walk home.

He reached across her to unlock the door. Shrinking back inside her seat belt, she was smothered for a moment in the warm cotton smell of his shirt, perfumed with cologne and barbecue smoke. He laughed at her. — Don't worry. I haven't got any designs on your virtue. I'll drive you home in a moment, or you can walk in your bare feet if you prefer it. Like I said, I just want to talk to you about something. I want to warn you about my grandfather, that's all. For your own good. He's got a big crush on you, he wants to give you presents – and why shouldn't he? But I thought you ought to know a bit more about him before you make up your mind whether to accept them.

He pushed the car door wide open and they listened to the muted, tickling noises the engine made as it cooled. — I don't even want his presents, Marina said. — Your mother knows that. I don't even take them.

— Well, just in case.

And he told her what the old man had been involved in, in the seventies and eighties, working in special operations for the South African Defence Force. — The details are pretty murky, Anthony said. — A lot of accusations were flying around.

Somehow the old man had got away with an amnesty – perhaps because he was already in his late sixties by then, retired to his farm. — I don't condemn him. I don't think you can condemn anything, unless you were there. Mum said there was no point in telling you – it's all old history now. He's just a sad old man. But I thought that you might like to know, that's all.

She meant to look it up on the Internet when she got home (Anthony had said that some of the stories were there if you searched for his grandfather's name), but she didn't. She lay in bed beside Gary, who was sound asleep, and eventually she fell asleep herself. By the time she woke, Gary was moving around in the kitchen downstairs, putting the kettle on for tea and preparing Liam's breakfast. Through the floor, she could hear Liam's questions and Gary's low-voiced responses – not so much answers as reassurances of his steady presence.

Marina felt burdened, as if she'd woken from a clinging, unpleasant dream. Once, when she was a girl, walking with Gary in the woods, they'd come across something inexplicable and horrible – the rotting head of some creature caught in the cleft branch of a tree, a chain of vertebrae dangling below it. Because the vertebrae looked like a long neck, she'd thought at first that it must be a goose or a swan that had got trapped somehow; then she saw teeth, and tufts of gristly fur stuck to the skull. Gary had poked at it with a stick. It was a mammal, perhaps a big stoat; Gary could only think that it must have been dropped from the sky by a bird of prey, the flesh falling away from the backbone as it decayed. Marina had looked at the thing coolly, but then as she walked on its reality had taken up residence inside her. There was no violent shock, only a settled change, and the realisation – a surprise – that you couldn't undo the knowledge of the thing with the same calm ease with which you had taken it in. And for a while afterwards everything she looked at had seemed unclean, had revealed a leering, repulsive side she'd never seen before. She thought with distaste now of the old man's soiled linen soaking in a bucket.

She couldn't forgive herself for her innocence, which seemed wilful in retrospect; she remembered how the old man had courted and flattered her. As soon as she'd heard the things that Anthony listed, she had no doubt that some of them were true – enough of them for it not to matter which. They must have been written on the old man's surface, she thought, but she'd been too ignorant to read them. Gary asked wasn't she going to work today? Marina didn't want to, but she didn't want to explain to Gary, either, so she dressed and took Liam to school, then went into the churchyard. Clouds blew across the patchy sunshine. A new grave was littered with dead flowers still wrapped in cellophane, sodden ribbons, a child's paper windmill. Already the old man would be missing her. He was probably telephoning right now, to find out where she was. She kept her mobile switched off. Should she go up to the house? Was that her duty? She had thought she might go into the church to pray for guidance, but as soon as she sat down in the churchyard that idea sickened her, too, as another fake.

Instead, she set out for Wendy's, wanting to talk to her. It was along the way that Anthony had driven the night before; less than ten minutes by car, but quite a walk. Wendy's house, rectangular and substantial, newly painted cream, was set back from the road; when Marina was halfway up the gravelled drive she caught sight of Wendy standing at one of the upstairs windows as if she were looking out for her, expecting her. Wendy waved urgently; moments later, she appeared at the front door in a white towelling bathrobe and flip-flops, her hair scraped back from her forehead under a stretch band. She hurried up to Marina, seizing her hands. Naked of its make-up, greasy with cleanser, her face looked dazzled and bewildered.

— Is he gone?

— I don't know, Marina said, thinking she must mean Anthony.

— What's extraordinary, Wendy hurried on, not in her usual mocking, drawling voice but exalted and excited, — is that I've always dreamed of it happening just like this. In the dream, it's always morning and overcast, I'm running a bath in the en suite and I get undressed, the tap's still running, everything's steamy. Then in the dream

53

I get this premonition that it's going to happen, right now – and that's when the phone rings and it's my useless brother, ringing to tell me that Dad's dead. But the dream's changed since Dad came to live here. Now it's always you instead, bringing the news. You're always coming up the drive, wearing your pink jacket – I see your red hair. While I was running my bath this morning, I looked out and saw you, and it was exactly like it was in the dream, so I just knew.

Marina calmed her down and explained that she hadn't seen the old man yet this morning, that as far as she knew he was fine. Although Wendy seemed to listen, she was still agitated. She asked Marina to wait while she dressed. Then they drove down into the village together, to check on him. Wendy never asked why Marina had come to see her, and her explanation was overtaken by events. The old man had died peacefully in his sleep. Almost peacefully. There was some evidence of a struggle with the bedclothes. He had fallen halfway out of the bed when they found him, with his head on the floor.

He did leave Marina the house in his will – he'd changed it only a few weeks before his death – but she wouldn't take it. The solicitors said that her refusal was unusual but not unprecedented; she had to sign a disclaimer in order to give the house back. Eventually, Wendy got builders into it, renovating from top to bottom, doing it up beautifully. Then she moved in herself and put her other place on the market. She tried to give Marina some money instead of the house, but Marina wouldn't touch a penny. It caused trouble between her and Gary. Gary didn't see why she shouldn't have something, and Marina's mother agreed: they could put it aside, in case Liam wanted to go to college later. But once Marina got an idea into her head there was no changing it. Gary knew that better than anyone. In the end, he went along with what she wanted.

Deeds Not Words

All the girls at St Clements loved Miss Mulhouse. Quite a few of them had loved her even before she broke windows in a shop in Oxford Street and was arrested as a suffragette. She was graceful and earnest and angularly thin, with a lot of very soft hair and large interesting pale eyes, the lids languidly heavy. Her intensity was of the smouldering and not the flaring kind, and she read Browning and Dante Gabriel Rossetti to the girls in her lessons. *I have been here before, / But when or how I cannot tell: / I know the grass beyond the door, / The sweet keen smell . . .*

After the news of her arrest had spread – someone's father had found her name in the newspapers – loving Miss Mulhouse became a kind of cult in the school and no one dared not belong. The girls decorated their desks in WSPU colours, purple and green and white, and stuck pictures of the Pankhursts inside their desk lids. They found out their teacher's first name, *Laura* – perhaps it had been in the list in the newspaper – and passed it around in hushed voices, like an initiation into occult knowledge. Fervently some of them began mugging up on suffragist politics; one of the day girls had a brother with a printing set, and they composed angry pamphlets with 'Believe and You Will Conquer' in big letters set crookedly on the front page, or 'Liberty and No Surrender.' All through prayers one morning, one of these pamphlets was drawing-pinned at the very centre of the honours board, where the names of distinguished alumnae were picked out in gold. Afterwards discussion surged around the groups of girls: had the teachers and the headmistress really not noticed their pamphlet? Or had they seen it and chosen to leave it there? Some of them were known to be sympathisers.

Edith Carew taught Latin, and approved in principle – of course – of votes for women, but was too sceptical to be an enthusiast for any political cause. Laura Mulhouse had always seemed vaguely comical to her, drifting through the corridors with her arms full of poetry books and her air of high-minded regret. Laura had such reserves of indignation over so many outrages, and seemed freshly astonished every day by the world's wickedness – though she could be petty over borrowed teacups in the staffroom. Edith thought that Laura played up to certain susceptible girls, too, encouraging them to worship her. Edith and the French teacher, Mr Briers, had called Laura privately the Lady of Shalott – it was Mr Briers's first shared joke with Edith, though they gave it up later when Laura was in prison. By that time, anyway, Edith wasn't giving Laura Mulhouse much thought. Her mind was all absorbed in lower things: she was drowning in her love affair with Fitzsimmon Briers.

Edith was thirty-four and lively and not bad-looking and had always expected to get married, but humiliatingly she had to own up to Fitz that this was her first experience of love – certainly of what she shyly called 'intimate relations'. Fitz was the most intelligent man Edith had ever got anywhere close to; his dry humour and his good taste, and his appreciation of her, changed her life as drastically as if she found footprints on an island where she'd been beginning to believe she was alone. Sometimes she felt this alteration so intensely that she imagined he must be leaving actual marks on her body, and looked for them after they'd spent time together. Fitz was heavy and shambolic, with black hair and a beard, and silky black hair on his chest. Edith was trim with a neat figure; she had dreaded that this body would bloom and fade under her clothes without any man ever knowing it. Unfortunately, and it was just her luck – the only thing to do with her luck, Edith thought, was to laugh at it – Fitz was married, with a child. He wouldn't talk about his wife, just said she was an invalid and didn't go out much. Edith had never seen her. People said she'd had a nervous collapse.

St Clements had moved recently into an eighteenth-century gentleman's residence built on the hillside above a seaside town on the south coast; the classrooms were wood-panelled and poky, and all the headmistress's energies were bent on raising funds for a modern science block. Every afternoon after the end of school, when she wasn't on duty and Fitz could get away, Edith climbed the back staircase in Old Court to the French office, hardly more than a cupboard under the roof, where French grammar books were kept along with spare chairs and editions of Racine and Victor Hugo. This staircase was forbidden to the girls. Fitz would be waiting for her, he would hurry her over the threshold, nuzzling her hands and her arms as if he was too hungry to delay. Then he'd lock the door behind them and lay out on the floorboards the blankets he'd brought from home, which smelled of mothballs. Sometimes rain drummed on the sloping roof, enclosing them, sometimes the sun baked down on it and their skins were slick with sweat. Edith could hardly believe that this French cupboard which had been so prosaically ordinary could transform itself into the scene of such revelations. After their intimacies, while she lay curled in the crook of his arm, he read to her out of *Phèdre* or Mme de Staël. He had a beautiful accent and got carried away with the sound of the words, Edith had to whisper to him to keep quiet. She was haunted by the perils of their situation, though she'd never been fearful in her life before. They might be found out, and she would be disgraced, they would both lose their jobs. Or she might conceive a child – though Fitz assured her that he 'knew what he was doing'.

Meanwhile word went round that Miss Mulhouse was on hunger strike in prison, and being force-fed: passion for the movement blew up fervidly among the girls. They asked permission to hold meetings in the common room. In the end the headmistress agreed, though not all her teachers supported her – and the meetings were so well attended they had to be moved into the refectory. Certain members of staff went along too. Crazes had swept the school before, Edith remembered – for automatic writing, or the novels of Marie Corelli; last winter half the girls were wearing crosses hidden under their blouses, and swapping scent bottles supposed to be filled with holy water. Fitz agreed with Edith that the force-feeding was barbaric, but he said that Laura Mulhouse had gone to Oxford Street intent on suffering: in another era she'd have been a Christian martyr. Police brutality only encouraged hysterical behaviour. Then two senior girls were suspended – there was a rumour they'd been planning to invade the local racecourse. Someone set fire to a pillar box in the high street, though probably this had nothing to do with the school.

At the end of one afternoon, when Edith and Fitz climbed the stairs to the French cupboard, its door was daubed with slogans in white paint. 'End this outrage now!' 'Stop the torture of women!'

In her shock Edith was confused for a moment. — Do they know about us?

— Don't be silly. It's nothing to do with us. It's those blasted suffragettes.

Fitz was right of course – it turned out the slogans were all over the place, the work of the girls who'd been suspended, and who'd crept back with a bucket of white-wash while the school was in afternoon lessons. He said Edith better not stay, there was bound to be uproar. Sick with her disappointment, she made her way downstairs.

61

All that was left for her now was to return to her lodgings, heat up her supper of leftover meat and vegetables and rice pudding over the paraffin lamp, prepare her lessons for the next day. I might as well be dead, she thought, crossing the school garden. The evening was tenderly sunlit and warm, and a little breeze turned the leaves of the young beech trees pale side out – but all its loveliness was wasted. She was waylaid by a fourth-former, a big-bosomed gushing girl called Ursula Smythe with a WSPU badge pinned to her lapel. Ursula was carrying a petition clipped to a board.

— Miss Carew, do you support votes for women? Will you sign the petition for our poor Miss Mulhouse?

Bad-temperedly Edith pushed the petition away. — For goodness' sake, Ursula, I've got tests to mark. I can't help what Miss Mulhouse chooses to do with her spare time. I suppose she knew what she was letting herself in for.

What good would it do anyone, Edith thought, for a dolt like Ursula Smythe to have the vote? What would she vote for? Hadn't she been one of the champions at automatic writing, filling whole exercise books with her nonsense?

After the incident with the whitewash, the school governors suspended the headmistress and certain teachers. The girls had worked themselves up by this time into such a state that when this news got around there were riots in the classrooms and it was impossible to impose any kind of discipline, or carry on with normal lessons.

The boarders tore up sheets to make sashes painted with the WSPU slogan, 'Deeds Not Words'. They called themselves 'irregulars' and barricaded themselves in the dormitories, threatening to jump out of the windows; on one occasion the police had to be called in. Parents who got wind of the disturbances came to carry their daughters off to safety. All this lasted for several weeks and it was hard to see where it would end – until the school holidays arrived, and then in August war was declared, and the WSPU announced from Pankhurst headquarters in Paris that it was abandoning its campaign for the duration.

One evening in September Miss Carew and Mr Briers met in the school grounds. They couldn't use the French cupboard any longer, because Mr Briers had resigned from his position at the school and been awarded a commission in the Queen's Royal West Surrey Regiment. All the furore of the summer had died down; girls in their white blouses paraded calmly, arm in arm, or chased one another squealing round the great cedar on the lawn. Some were already knitting socks for soldiers. Edith and Fitz were on a bench at a turn in the path, tucked behind some holly bushes; when Edith raised her voice Fitz warned her that the girls were watching, but she hardly cared. He had his back half turned, with his shoulder in its ghastly khaki hunched against her, as if he were only enduring their conversation. His black hair, which had been carelessly unkempt in the days when he read Racine to her, was now shorn close; where his ears stuck out from his scalp the skin was reddened and raw.

— How can you give yourself to this beastly war? she raged. — I can't believe you don't see through it all as I do. You never had these militarist opinions before. Isn't it all so foul? Don't you hate the idea of all this death and pain?

With heavy patience he tried to explain. — Whatever my opinions are, how can I stay at home teaching French to little girls, when other men are giving their lives out there?

She thought that if only she could touch him, she could win him back.

— What does your wife think?

He turned his hooded eyes on her, gleaming in righteous anger. — Don't speak about my wife.

Then Edith guessed that he had a picture in his mind like a sentimental postcard, of his wife standing waving farewell to him as he went off to war, hidden half out of sight behind a curtain at a window, perhaps with the child in her arms – whatever it was, girl or boy. Of course Edith had no place in this sacred scene, contaminating it. She jumped up from the bench as if she had to save herself from his new patriotic stupidity. But no matter how she saw through his condemnation, she couldn't escape it: he had power over her, because of what had happened in the French cupboard. It was another sentimental postcard: she was unchaste, she had forfeited the white flower of a blameless life, she wasn't the kind of woman a man would go to war for. Fitz was allowed to think this if he liked. She walked away from him through the garden without looking back once, and went inside the school to collect her books – she had ten minutes, thankfully, before classes started. She needed to sit for a moment in the classroom, to collect herself, because her legs were shaking.

And on her way up the back stairs she met Laura Mulhouse coming down. Laura had spent the summer at home with her mother, recovering from her ordeal in prison; now she'd quietly resumed her teaching. The girls hadn't made any great fuss over her. The headmistress and all the other teachers had been reinstated, no one spoke now about the madness of last term. Edith stopped to let her pass on the narrow staircase. Laura didn't look as intense as she used to: she was oddly stooped and her hair lay dead flat and her complexion was lustreless and clammy. Edith remembered what she'd read about force-feeding: the India-rubber tube pushed up the women's noses, the indignity and dreadful pain and the choking and vomiting. Both of them were broken, Edith thought. In their shame, they could hardly bear to look at each other.

One Saturday Morning

Carrie was alone in the house. It was a Saturday in the mid-1960s, and her parents were out shopping: she was ten years old, and doing her piano practice. She had borrowed her parents' alarm clock and put it on top of the piano to time herself – she had so many twenty-minute practices to make up, it seemed as though she'd have to sit there forever. Sometimes she just stared at the clock stonily, letting her fingers wander at random around the notes. Her younger brother, Paul, had a game of cricket going outside with his gang of friends, on the stretch of worn grass enclosed by railings that was a kind of garden for the whole terrace, although only the children used it. The chock of the ball against the bat and the boys' voices calling to one another sounded dreamy at this distance, travelling across the road through the summer heat. Every so often a boy appealed – 'Owzat! – with sudden violence. Carrie shuddered; it was still cool indoors and she wished she had her cardigan on. This room at the front of the house was always dark, because of the horse chestnut tree outside the window. They called it the dining room, though they used it for dining only on special occasions, or when her mother had a dinner party; mostly, they watched television in here. A dinner party was planned, in fact, for that night, and the room seemed braced in anticipation: the notes Carrie played fell into an alert silence.

The television was in a corner, opposite a low couch covered in olive-green cotton; Carrie's mother had made the couch covers and also the floor-length curtains and the pelmet at the window, in mustard-yellow velvet. All of the ground floor – the dining room and the kitchen and the hall – was laid with black-and-white Vinolay tiles, stuck to sheets of hardboard nailed over the old wood floor. Carrie's parents had done this themselves, in the evenings and at weekends, when her father wasn't at work – he taught in a secondary modern school. Not many people in those days were keen to live in these dilapidated Georgian terraced houses, so a schoolteacher and his wife could afford one, if they had imagination and were able to do it up themselves. Carrie's mother had a vision of the house she wanted, elegant and arty. A bulb in a Japanese white-paper globe was suspended on a long flex from the high ceiling. Carrie had turned on this light when she came downstairs to do her practice, and in the daylight it glowed weakly and inhospitably.

She was working through the exercises in a book called *A Dozen a Day*. The twelfth and last exercise in each section was 'Fit as a Fiddle and Ready to Go', but Carrie had worn out all the hopefulness she'd felt when she first started piano lessons. She knew that she wasn't particularly good, and that piano wasn't the answer she'd hoped for, to what was unsolved in herself. There was something slapdash in the way her mind connected with the sounds that her fingers were making. Also, an uncomfortable thing had happened recently in relation to her piano teacher, who was kind and sensible, with a bosom that quivered in stretch polo necks. A few weeks ago Carrie had lost a letter that she had written to her best friend, Susan, and she was afraid that she'd dropped it at her piano teacher's house, though she wasn't sure. Her teacher hadn't said anything about it, but that didn't mean she hadn't found it.

The letter was a joke, one in a series that Carrie and Susan had been writing to each other, full of rude words and innuendo, half learned from the playground and half invented. In the letters they addressed each other as Dug-less and Fanny, and traded insults. *Dear Fanny, Guess what? P.A. told me that you asked him to show you his thingy. He said you really liked it, and wanted to touch it! Then you cried when he wouldn't let you. Boo-hoo!* Outwardly, Carrie and Susan were not at all like the clowning raucous characters in the letters: they were quiet girls, shy and hard-working. The boy in their jokes was always the same one: a fat boy in their class, who was their enemy. He banged down their desk lids on their heads, pretended to waft away their bad smells, asked if they were wearing itchy knickers. The letters had seemed richly and mysteriously funny, until the joy was tainted by Carrie's having to imagine her piano teacher reading one.

Bitterly she addressed herself, frown lines cut deep between her eyes, to one of Bartók's children's pieces, breaking it down as she was supposed to, practising the left hand first, over and over. There was a relief in pounding the repeated chords, which were neither contented nor plangent. Her right hand lay curled in her lap, palm upward, a useless and discarded thing, and she swung her legs under the piano stool as she concentrated: a sharp-faced little scrap of a girl, blotted with freckles, straight hair pushed out of the way behind sticking-out ears. She looked like her father's side of the family – thin and strong-boned – and not like her mother, who was opulently attractive: shapely, with wide hazel eyes and a full mouth. It was Paul who looked like their mother.

Above the dining-room fireplace was a gilt-framed mirror that their mother had found in a junk shop and repaired; she had also made lamps out of old glass demijohns and pottery bottles, with her own silk shades. The grate in the fireplace was filled all year round with dried flowers and a gold paper fan: no one wanted real fires when you could have central heating. In photographs now, those arty sixties rooms look unexpectedly austere; their effects seem sparse and rickety, amateurish, in comparison with the fat tide of spending and decorating that came later. But that innocence is appealing, and not incongruous with the high-ceilinged Georgian rooms, always painted white.

The doorbell rang, tearing into Carrie's solitude. She felt herself reprieved – she had done almost an hour's practice, and there was still tomorrow. It might be her parents, back already from Sainsbury's, or Paul, coming in from across the road to look for another ball or to get a drink of water. When he ran in from his games he sometimes drank straight from the tap in the kitchen, making a great show of his wild heat and thirst, cocking his head under the flow, letting the water soak his hair, his eyes rolling back as if he were delirious with physical effort. Carrie caught sight of her reflection in another mirror, above the Pembroke table in the hall, with its bowl of unmatched gloves left over from winter and its jug filled with silvery dried honesty. The outer front door stood open, as it always did in the daytime; the inner door was made of rippled glass. A man was leaning against the glass on the other side, his bulk blocking the light. He was peering inside through his cupped hands to see if anyone was at home.

Carrie dreaded any encounter with a stranger and wished she hadn't let herself be seen. Suffering, she fumbled with the lock, as the man stepped back. When she swung the door open, she discovered that he wasn't a stranger after all but someone who didn't come to the house often enough for her to have recognised his outline. Dom Smith was a friend of her parents' who had moved to another city some time ago, to a new job at a

71

university. Her parents would be so disappointed to miss Dom. He was a favourite of theirs, clever and handsome, an anthropologist, with a young family. Carrie's mother talked about him in the cherishing tone that she reserved for certain people she admired, mostly men, mostly just out of reach on the margins of their acquaintance; she liked the idea of Dom's life, with its aura of bohemianism and its promise of good conversation. She liked his wife, Helen, too, but they'd seen less of her. Once, Helen had lived with Dom among the tribal peoples in Assam. Now, when he came visiting friends, she often stayed at home with her babies.

Dom puzzled down at Carrie, perhaps only vaguely remembering her existence, certainly not her name. In his shabby reefer jacket, he seemed too warmly dressed for the summer day; she could smell his sweat. If only her parents had been at home, she could have tagged on behind their welcome, basking invisibly at the edge of all the talk. Her father enjoyed their noisy quarrels over music (Dom liked classical, her father liked jazz), in which neither of them gave an inch. Dom had the kind of physique that makes a man seem fearless – he was huge and rumpled, with untidy black curls and a beard, a big affable voice. You could easily imagine him living in a hut in Assam, with people who kept the bones of their ancestors under the floor. Actually, he was fairly diffident and awkward. He told Carrie that he was in town for a couple of days, looking up old friends. Were her parents anywhere around?

— They're out at the shops, she said. You could come in and wait.

He hesitated and cast a look back into the street, almost as if he were being pursued.

— How long d'you think they'll be?

They would be back very soon, Carrie reassured him, eager to coax him inside. Yet as soon as he stepped across the threshold into the dim interior, she felt how inadequate she was to entertain him. Her parents' friends might play significant roles in her imagination, but left alone with them she had nothing to offer. Dom's towering presence was confounding; he stood with his back to the hall mirror, obliterating her reflection and surveying the place, as if to remind himself where he was. They both seemed at a loss.

— Were you playing the piano? he asked politely. — Why don't you go ahead?

It would be unbearable to play while he was listening. Carrie gabbled something about reading her book and fled upstairs; her cowardice was crucifying. But as soon as her parents came back from the shops the tide of their pleased sociability would lift her with it; she'd be all right. Skulking behind the open door of the playroom, she listened to Dom moving around downstairs. They called this room the playroom because there was a table-tennis table in it, which her father had rescued when the school was throwing it out. Her mother kept her sewing machine there, too, and the table was spread with the cut-out and pinned pieces of a dress she was making for one of the ladies she sewed for. Dom went into the kitchen and must have sat still for a bit because she couldn't hear him. Then he pushed back a chair and began pacing again, in and out of the dining room, back to the kitchen; Carrie felt guiltily responsible for his restlessness.

She took off her sandals so that she wouldn't make a sound; he mustn't know that she was wandering upstairs, prickling with consciousness of his wanderings below. Several times she tiptoed to the windows in the lounge, to see whether her parents' car was pulling up; its continuing absence was a physical pain. After a while she got out her shoebox full of the collectible cards that came free with packets of tea, then sat down at the table-tennis table and began doggedly pasting these into their places in her albums. She was saving British Butterflies and Great Engineers. Dom meandered into the dining room again. It was strange that a grown man could be reduced to the listlessness of a child, waiting for something that didn't come.

He sat down at the piano and began to play. The piece was much too advanced to be in any of the books she had, so it must have been something he knew by heart. Carrie put down her pot of paste and crept out of the playroom, sitting at the top of the stairs to listen, hugging her stomach, feeling the music for once as if it were inside her. It was the tiny scope of her Bartók piece, she saw now, that made it suitable for children. This different music rolled and rippled up and down the notes, joyous and mournful, lingering and delaying, holding back with painful sweetness. Carrie was in awe of Dom Smith's adult competence, so rich in understanding; she couldn't imagine attaining it in any lifetime.

Then he broke off abruptly in the middle of the piece, pushing back the piano stool as if he were angry with it and striding out into the hall, where he hesitated before calling upstairs. — Hello?

He was going to go; she should never have tried to keep him there in the first place – the only surprise was his even remembering that she was in the house. When he called, she didn't answer right away, not wanting him to know that she'd been listening from the stairs. And at that very moment her parents arrived home from the supermarket: she heard their voices first, then a key in the lock and the noise rolling in from the street. Her mother exclaimed in shock at finding Dom Smith in her hall, on the point of leaving.

— Dom! What a lovely surprise! Did Carrie let you in?

— I was just about to give up on you, he said.

Carrie bounded downstairs, to be present at the happy greetings. She knew that her mother would be quickly calculating, standing among the plastic carriers from the supermarket, rearranging her plans to make room for Dom, running through what preparation was still needed for the dinner party. Her timetable leading up to these events was tightly organised, and she worked through it with fierce energy and efficiency, but she could make lightning adjustments, too. All this time she was showing Dom her brightly delighted face. She was genuinely pleased that he had come.

— I told him to wait, Carrie said, hanging on to her mother's arm and stretching out her feet in the new ballet moves that Susan had taught her. She was performing for him now that she was safe. — I knew you wouldn't be long.

— I'm down for a few days, Dom said. — I came for a rugby game and I thought I'd catch up with people.

He stood awkwardly in their way in his thick dark coat; it was hard to believe that such marvellous music had poured out of him only a few minutes earlier. Carrie's father, his extreme thinness and height making him look martyred under the weight of more shopping bags, was thankful for male company after a morning at the supermarket. Paul ran in from across the road and began hunting through the carriers for a packet of crisps, glancing only once at their visitor, then hurrying out again, fairly oblivious of his family's social life. Carrie's father asked about the rugby, while her mother turned on the coffee percolator and unpacked the perishables into the fridge. The grown-ups sat down around the kitchen table to drink their coffee, and Carrie pulled up a stool to sit beside her mother, delighted with Dom's presence now, as if it were her own achievement. Her mother tore open a packet of chocolate truffles in his honour, but he shook his head. Carrie was allowed just one. No doubt they'd been intended for the dinner party.

— So how are things? her father cheerfully asked.

— I have to tell you straight away, Dom said.

* * *

Helen, his wife, had died suddenly of meningitis in the spring. She had gone to bed one night complaining of backache, Dom had called an ambulance the next morning, and she had died at the hospital the following day. Now Helen's mother was helping Dom look after the children, because he had to work. Carrie's family hadn't heard anything about this. In those days, news didn't travel so fast; lots of people didn't even have telephones. And her parents didn't really have many friends in common with the Smiths. In fact, after this one momentous visit when he brought his news, Carrie's family didn't see Dom again for a long time.

He stayed that day for hours, sitting with Carrie's parents at the kitchen table. Carrie crept upstairs, to be where she couldn't hear them talking in their stricken, changed voices, but she couldn't get rid of the terrible knowledge that Dom had brought; it seemed to be stuck inside her, in her stomach or her throat. Her bedroom was high up in the attic, under the roof baking in the sun, hot even with the windows wide open; in summer the weedy, sour smell of the rush matting on the floor was overpowering. She knelt on it, punishing herself, until its corded pattern was printed as red welts in the flesh of her bare knees. If only she hadn't let Dom Smith into the house. She tried not to remember him announcing his news, in those oddly hearty, premeditated sentences; his words cut across the bright air of her bedroom in stark flashes, darkening it. Her parents' jolly hospitality had been stalled mid-gesture; Carrie saw her mother holding the percolator at a slant but not pouring, surprising tears brimming into her hazel eyes, as if they had been waiting for this moment, close beneath the surface. Her father, in his role as the man of the house, was the first to struggle, heroically clumsy, to say something. Her mother had just let out a cry, as if it were she who was wounded.

Carrie took everything to heart. She was earnest and susceptible, suffering easily. But it wasn't exactly pity for Helen Smith or her husband or children that overwhelmed her as she knelt in her bedroom; it was something more selfish and self-protective. She wished fiercely that she'd never learned about Helen's death. Helen didn't seem the right person to be singled out. She had been tiny and plump and hopeful, with soft brown hair and a pleasant ringing voice. But now the idea of death closed on her in Carrie's imagination, like a trap. Her image and her name had been transformed by Dom's announcement, and were framed with sorrow, could never be dissociated from it. Helen's children had still been small when the Smiths moved away; Carrie had hardly known them. Before the Smiths left, the two families had gone for a walk together in some woods, and Carrie remembered that Dom had carried his younger daughter in a backpack, which wasn't common then. The thong had broken on one of Helen's sandals and she'd had to keep bending down to adjust it. After the walk, they had gone back to the Smiths' flat for tea, and Helen had fried Scotch pancakes, which they ate hot with butter. The flat was on a steep hill, overlooking the river and the docks below; it was shabby and comfortable, untidy with books and baby apparatus. Carrie's mother had said on the way home that the flat could have been made very nice, but Helen Smith wasn't interested in that sort of thing. She'd said this defensively, as if Helen had actually reproached her for her frivolous concern with appearances.

This morning, the memory of that walk had been jumbled carelessly among all Carrie's other memories; now it had to be separated from the rest, darkened with foreboding. She felt relieved that those smitten children lived in another city, far away. The sensations of her long vigil alone with Dom Smith in the house were vividly present still; she was shrivelled and humiliated by the foolish excitement she had felt at keeping him waiting, then offering her family to him like a bright gift. Peering in through the glass door, then blundering around in the shadows downstairs, Dom was turned into a figure of dread by what had happened to him. He was set apart, just as his wife had been set apart – except that it was worse with Dom, because he persisted, discomforting in all his living bulk, putting himself in the way of Carrie's thoughts when she tried to be rid of him. She longed to hear the door shut behind him and for the dinner-party preparations to be resumed, however belatedly – for the whole ordinary process of living to start into motion again, downstairs in the kitchen.

* * *

It was a lovely evening, very still. The house filled up with the smell of meat stewing slowly in wine. Slanting yellow light, thick with dancing midges, pooled under the horse chestnuts outside. The floor-length sash windows were thrown up in the lounge, and after the guests had finished eating they came upstairs to sit there in the twilight, smoking and drinking. Two men started a game of table tennis in the playroom, slamming the ball down hard, exploding with shouts of triumph or defeat. There was jazz music on the gramophone in the lounge, and a blackbird competed in a tree outside; some of the guests came out to smoke on the white-painted wrought-iron balcony, where Carrie's mother grew nicotiana and petunias and white lobelia, in pots and in the halves of a barrel sawn in two. Cigarette smoke and the smell of flowers, together with the uninterpretable mingled voices and laughter from inside the room, floated up to where Carrie watched, unseen, from the open window in her parents' bedroom on the floor above.

She and her brother were supposed to be asleep in their rooms in the attic. But Carrie was spying on the dinner party and Paul was sitting up in bed in his thin cotton pyjamas, his skin darkly tanned from the days outdoors, his hair bleached a striking yellow gold. Carrie knew that he was writing his weather report in a notebook – sunny, some high cumulus, 68°F, no precipitation – and flipping back through its pages to where things got more interesting: his record-low temperature for the year, heaviest rainfall, days of hail or thunder. He would be murmuring certain favourite words over to himself, incantatory: *the leaden sky promised an early fall of snow.*

Carrie had found the stupid letter that she'd thought was lost, tucked into the pocket of a cardigan put away in her drawer. She had dived on it with a little private cry of pain, then torn it up quickly without reading it, burying the fragments in her wastepaper bin. Of course she was relieved; certain scenes at her piano teacher's house could now be wiped clean of the taint of her teacher's knowledge. Yet her relief was trivial, because the problem of the lost letter had been displaced by something quite incommensurate with it. Resolutely, Carrie refused to let thoughts of the Smiths into the foreground of her attention. At least Dom was gone now, and she could begin to forget about him; the time they'd spent in the house together shamed her.

Her mother had tried to persuade Dom to come back for the dinner party, and he'd promised to think about it, but she'd said afterwards that she was sure he wouldn't come – it would be unbearable under the circumstances for him to mix with strangers, or people he hardly knew. Carrie couldn't tell from her mother's voice whether she was glad that Dom wouldn't come, or sorry. But surely he would have ruined things – what could they have laughed at, if he'd brought his weight of sadness in among them? His visit had disrupted her mother's plans, but still she had got everything ready on time, working under pressure with a severe, set face: the table had been laid beautifully with its blue-and-brown-checked cloth and red-stemmed glasses and red paper napkins; the glazed vol-au-vents were filled and ready for the oven; the chocolate pudding was set in its palisade of sponge fingers, piped with whipped cream; the candles were on the table with their box of matches.

In the half-dark now, feeling the evening air against her nakedness under her nightdress, Carrie fingered the objects on her mother's dressing table, so well known they seemed like parts of her own self: the amber necklace with its knotted waxy thread, the prickly dried sea horse someone had brought from Greece, a cylinder needle case of polished wood, a bottle of the Basic Dew that her mother used on her face. The coral brooch, with its fine gold safety chain and extra pin, had belonged to her mother's own mother; a black lacquer box was painted with forget-me-nots and had a poem pasted inside the lid. This bedroom was never as perfectly tidy as the rooms downstairs. There were stray halfpennies and dressmaker's pins in the dust on the dressing table, neglected letters in manila envelopes were propped against the mirror, and one of Paul's football boots was wrapped in a plastic bag, waiting to be repaired. Some meaning was hidden in these mute things Carrie touched: twisting the top off the needle case, she tested the blunt ends of a few rusty needles, pressing hard and then harder, until the needles made white dents in her fingertips.

Then, when she looked out of the window again to check on the party, she saw to her horror that Dom Smith was standing out on the balcony below, with his back to her. So he had turned up after all. It was Dom, she realised now, who had been playing table tennis with her father, yelling and cursing and shouting with glee, throwing himself about the room as if the only thing he cared about was winning. Now he was alone, leaning hunchbacked over the railing in the shadows between the two lit windows, his shoulders broad in his checked shirt, whose sleeves were rolled up, businesslike, to the elbows. While she watched, he threw his cigarette down into the street. Carrie's mother stepped out onto the balcony through one of the windows; the noise of the party carried on in the room behind her. Carrie saw that her mother didn't really know Dom well, and was uncertain whether she ought to approach him. Her sleeveless white dress, which she had made herself, gleamed in the twilight. She must have kicked off her white shoes in the lounge; it was one of the things she did when she was tipsy. Hesitant, she moved towards him, and he turned his head to look at her.

— Dom, I don't know what to say. Poor, lovely Helen. It's too awful.

Where they were standing, between the two windows, they weren't visible from inside the lounge, but Carrie saw what happened next. Dom grabbed hold of her mother – not suavely and sexily, like one of those flirty men who were always grabbing at her, but clumsily, half smothering her. The top of her head only just came up to his chin, but he squeezed her tightly and nuzzled under her ear, as if he wanted to burrow down into her.

Her mother was taken by surprise; she staggered backwards under Dom's weight and at the same time patted his shoulder as if she were comforting him. He was speaking but the words were muffled, because his face was buried in her neck.

— You've had too much to drink, she said tenderly. — You're not making any sense.

For a while the two of them clung together, circling slowly on the creaky planks of the balcony as if they were dancing. He was pressing the huge palm of his hand against her head, stroking her tousled hair, clasping her head against his chest, kissing the top of it, kissing her ear. Carrie felt as if she weren't really present at the scene; she was disembodied. She believed that, even if they'd looked up to where she was craning out of the window above them, they wouldn't have been able to see her. Then her mother, with her hand flat on Dom's chest, was pushing him away in the teasing, charming way she pushed away the other men. — I'm so sorry, she said. — I'm so sorry, Dom, but I can't. Quietly Carrie stepped away from the window and went upstairs. She pictured herself making a joke at breakfast the next day about her mother dancing on the balcony with Dom Smith, and then she knew she mustn't, and grew hot with the memory of the rude letter, her wrong judgement of what was funny and what was shaming.

Paul was still sitting up in bed in the room next to hers. He snapped his notebook shut when she came in. — Get out, he said. — I'm doing something.

84

Carrie ignored him and stretched out her leg, pulling up her nightdress to her knees, pointing her toes and practising ballet moves in the narrow space between Paul's bed and his collection of empty cereal boxes stacked against the wall. She had given up her ballet lessons; she wasn't really any better at ballet than at the piano. An insect flew in through the open window and landed on the cover of Paul's book. — I can see his eyes, he said, peering closely. — They're like little blobs of ink, gold ink. He's looking right back at me.

Then their mother, barefoot, was standing in the doorway. — What are you up to? she said crossly. — You two are supposed to be in bed.

But she didn't seem to be in any hurry to get back to her guests. She began picking up the clothes that Paul had dropped on the floor and folding them. Carrie kept very still, with one foot pointing and her arms curved in an arabesque above her head. It occurred to her that her mother was afraid of Dom Smith, too. She didn't want to return downstairs, where he was waiting with his loss and his hunger for consolation.

— Look, Mummy, Paul said. — Come and look at this.

The three of them bent together over the insect, whose frail folded wings were transparent and dark-veined. Its long green body curled and uncurled lasciviously. — What an extraordinary creature, their mother said. Pressing close against her, Carrie breathed in her perfume, and the wine and smoke on her hot skin; the white dress smelled of ironing. Paul blew gently at the insect, which swayed on its threads of legs. Their happiness in that moment was almost too much – its precariousness squeezed Carrie's chest like a tight band. A breeze stirred in the horse chestnut trees beyond the casement windows, and a street lamp glowing through the foliage was a glassy lozenge, like a sucked barley sugar. Already Carrie hardly knew if she'd actually seen Dom dancing on the balcony with her mother, or if that had only happened in her imagination, a vision of what consolation might be – something headlong and reckless and sweet, unavailable to children.

Experience

When my marriage fell apart one summer, I had to get out of the little flat in Kentish Town, where I had been first happy and then sad. I arranged to live for a few months in another woman's house; she let me stay there rent-free, because she was going to America and wanted someone to keep an eye on things. I didn't know Hana very well; she was a friend of a friend. I found her intimidating – she was tall and big-boned and gushing, with a high forehead and a curvaceous strong jaw, a mass of chestnut-coloured curls. But I liked the idea of having her three-storey red-brick London town house all to myself.

She was generous when we met to sort out arrangements, telling me to make myself at home, entertain my friends, use her iMac and her Wi-Fi, help myself to anything I needed in the kitchen, and sleep in her bed. (— The bed's wonderfully comfortable, she said.) A woman would come in twice a week to clean, and

I didn't have to pay for that either. We sat at the counter in Hana's kitchen, drinking coffee and eating baklava from a cardboard box – left over from a dinner party the night before along with the remains of a salad wilting in its dressing, glasses with dregs of red wine by the sink, the taint of cigarette smoke. Hana had just showered, and her damp hair was twisted in a clip on top of her head; her heated skin gave off the strong smell of her perfume or her shower gel. A crumb of baklava stuck to her mouth. I guessed that she was in her early forties: the flesh was puffy under her eyes and at the corners of her lips; she might have had work done on her nose. I was twenty-eight, and she made me feel inexperienced, although I had been married for six years. She wore a bright yellow kimono embroidered with a dragon, and a heavy ivory bangle on her wrist. — I know, she said guiltily, grimacing and twisting it on her arm when she thought I was staring at it. — I shouldn't wear it; it's a sin. But it's an antique. I tell myself that these elephants would be long dead anyway.

There were no curtains on the windows of that house, not even in the bedrooms. At first, I found this unbearable. I undressed for bed in the bathroom; I got into bed in the dark. But after a while I began to get used to it. This was how Hana lived her life – flamboyantly on display, careless of who might be watching. I didn't flatter myself that anyone was watching me. Or if they were watching, they thought I was something I was not, so it didn't matter. They thought I was the owner of that house, with its big, bare rooms and wood floors and rugs and few, distinctive items of furniture: a retro armchair in tubular steel and black leather, a long glass-topped dining table, two antique mirrors framed with gilded Cupids bearing rose garlands. I've never had that kind of money, or anything like it. I think Hana made her money by dealing in art – there were paintings on all the walls – though some of the phone calls that came for her seemed to be related to the film business.

I moved in with a couple of boxes of things I'd salvaged from my marriage. What I'd really wanted was to walk out of the flat with nothing, shedding it all behind me as cleanly as a skin. The little collection of totems that I took with me everywhere – pebbles from a certain beach, some framed photographs, my dead mother's empty perfume bottle – looked like rubbish when I spread them out in Hana's bedroom, so I hid them away again. I told myself that this house was a good place for me, temporarily: this nowhere where I was nobody. When the woman came in to clean, I went out and walked around on Primrose Hill or went to a museum, if it was raining – it rained a lot that summer. My husband had given me some money in exchange for my share of the things we'd bought together (fridge, television, sofa, bed), and I was trying to make it last as long as possible. Hana had told me to help myself to what was in the freezer, so I ate through the odds and ends of food she had in there, including things I'd never tasted before – veal saltimbocca, shrimp in teriyaki sauce and jerk chicken.

When the money runs out, I thought, I'll start looking for work.

On rainy days I wandered from room to room in that big house, cocooned by the rushing, persistent sound of the rain sluicing across the slate roof, over-flowing in the gutters and downpipes. At midday the light outside was blue, and the panes in the tall windows seemed liquefied; I switched on all the lamps. I made myself coffee and carried it with me to the window, so that the steam from my mug misted the glass; the television flickered and capered, but I couldn't distract myself from the rain's urgency, as if it were something happening. I had thought that I would forget about Hana once she was out of the house, but moving around inside the shapes of her life, I found myself more power-fully impressed by her than I had been when she was present. The wardrobes full of her clothes stood in for her: velvet trousers and brocade jackets, an evening dress of pleated chiffon with a sequinned bodice – every-thing padded and sculpted, each outfit a performance in itself.

There were attic rooms at the top of the house and one of these was locked. Hana had emptied out drawers and cupboards to make space for me, so I guessed that she had tidied everything personal away into this room. I came across the key accidentally, in a kitchen drawer beside some tea towels; those attic rooms had the original door fittings and this was a long iron key, like something in a novel or a pantomime. At the time, I hardly regis-tered seeing it. Then it began to weigh on my mind, and one afternoon when I had nothing better to do, I took it upstairs to try it in the lock. I feel ashamed of this now, needless to say. I think I felt that because I was nobody, my slipping inside Hana's privacy wouldn't count as a real intrusion. And she'd left the key lying around, hadn't she? Anyway, I only meant to take a quick look.

The room was heaped surprisingly high with stuff, as if she'd been using it for storage for a long time. There were the clothes and shoes and bags filled with accessories and old make-up that I'd expected. There were also paintings – speculations that hadn't paid off, perhaps? – propped, sometimes two- or three-deep, against the walls, their faces turned away as if in disgrace. Two new mattresses were still in their polythene. Art objects – ceramics and ethnic souvenirs and bits of sculpted wood – were muddled on the floor with a food processor and china dinner plates, a steam cleaner and a broken chandelier with tangled crystals. Suitcases were piled on top of hi-fi speakers and an old computer; a black wetsuit was flung dramatically in a corner over surfboards and camping gear. There were boxes filled with DVDs and those big glossy books – biographies and cookbooks – that people give as presents and no one reads. I stepped inside the room. The air was thick with the heat that had collected under the roof and loud with the noise of the rain running down the far side of the sloping ceiling. It was like stepping into a cave. I felt as if I'd found my way into the inner workings of the house, or of Hana.

Boxes and plastic bags were crammed with papers: letters and postcards and notebooks, photographs, nothing in any kind of order – yellowing letters stuffed in with recent bank statements. I just poked around at first; I wasn't really reading anything. There were a lot of business papers, anyway, which didn't mean much to me, though the sums of money were startling. Even without touching the DVDs I could see that they were porn and the kind of hard-core horror films I couldn't watch: she had left the art films and romcoms downstairs for me. I picked up a heart-shaped box covered in padded red satin. Inside, nestled under a wad of black tissue, were scraps of scarlet lace underwear, furry hand-cuffs, fishnets, and a vibrator, as bald and blatant as a medical appliance; I put the lid back on hastily. But this stuff was ordinary, wasn't it? Everybody did it. What was the matter with me that I didn't take it for granted, that my heart beat stickily, as if the little sex kit had somehow made a fool of me? Kneeling on the bare boards, I started reading my way through the contents of a plastic bag.

One of the expensive leather-bound notebooks was a kind of diary. It began and broke off abruptly, without dates. Hana had become involved with a man named Julian. She wrote about him in a big, looping hand that filled up two ruled lines at a time, dotting her 'i's with circles, using a lot of asterisks and private code words and exclamation marks. Everything was 'amazing' or 'terrible'. 'I knew this was going to happen,' she wrote, 'from the first moment he walked into the party that night.' Julian told her that he couldn't get enough of her, that he was desperate for her, that he wanted her all over again as soon as he'd had her. They were at some dinner where they had to pretend not to know each other, ended up having sex in the bathroom. A line of dots, and then more exclamation marks. 'He hurts me and frightens me, but it's the best s*x ever.' Along with the sex, there was some lengthy analysis of Julian's personality. The two of them were very alike, Hana thought. They 'both had this ambition burning them up' and 'a lot of imagination'; also they 'needed to be free'. But a few pages on she was 'starting to see through him' – how moody he was, how he always had to be the centre of attention. 'Of course it's terrible about the children,' she wrote. They'd had a blissful weekend away together and swum naked in the sea, f****d in the shower. 'Now he's gone back to S and I feel like shit.' Hana made scenes, crawled to him on her knees, begged him to stay. 'J came round at three in the morning and I let him in, couldn't help myself. Then X and you know what. Crazy with love all over again. He makes me so happy.' These were the last words in the notebook.

I've never lived, I thought, as I knelt there, reading with my legs cramped underneath me, aware of the rain as if it were drumming on my skin. I've never lived: the words ran in my head. Life was garish and ruthless and exaggerated, and I'd never really had it – I was like one of those child brides in history whose marriage was annulled by the Pope because it wasn't consummated.

Of course, mine had been consummated in the ordinary sense. But even when my husband told me that he wanted us to separate, even when he told me that he wasn't in love with me any more, and that he'd better keep the flat because I wouldn't be able to afford the rent by myself, I hadn't ranted or thrown pans at him. (Hana had thrown a pan full of boiling pasta at Julian once. She'd missed, but the water had splashed his leg and scalded him, and then he'd hit her, and then they'd XXX: 'I'm covered in bruises this morning and feel fantastic, though I know it's crazy.')

My husband was intelligent and read a lot of books about history and politics; he worked as a policy officer for a borough-regeneration strategy. Whenever we quarrelled he didn't raise his voice but explained why I was wrong with a fixed, reasonable smile, tapping his foot under the table. We had once enjoyed visiting the Wren churches together, and we'd gone to evening classes to learn Greek, because there was an unspoiled Greek island that we visited whenever we could get away. When he asked me to move out, I didn't scream that I wouldn't be able to bear my life without him, because I knew that I probably could bear it. In the months before we separated, I noticed that he kept moving my toiletries off the shelf in the bathroom, onto the windowsill, as if they were already redundant. He and I had too much irony to take our lives as earnestly as Hana took hers. Viewed coldly from outside, how silly Hana's affair was and how demeaning, with its hysteria and its banal props. But who wanted to view things coldly, from outside?

And then one morning, when I was still in my pyjamas because I didn't have anything to get dressed for, the door phone buzzed in the kitchen. I thought it might be a delivery for Hana – she was buying things in California and shipping them home.

It was a man's voice, placatory and peremptory at once. — Hana? It's Julian. I have to pick up some stuff.

— Hana's not at home, I said.

He sounded taken aback but not disappointed. — Who are you, then?

— I'm living here.

When I opened the door to Julian, he didn't look at all as I'd imagined Hana's lover. He must have been several inches shorter than she was, to begin with: wiry, with a neat pixie face, a high forehead under a receding hairline, and a taut smile. He had a child in tow, a boy of eight or nine, with the same sandy colouring and quizzically interrogating look – only the child seemed puny and lethargic, while Julian exuded a kind of restless satisfaction. He rose and fell while we talked, elastic on the balls of his feet in their youthful trainers. I explained that I was staying in Hana's house while she was away. Julian said that he was an old friend of Hana's and needed to pick up some gear he'd left with her, a tent and sleeping bags.

— I'm taking the kids camping.

I did remember seeing a tent in the attic, but of course I couldn't tell him that. The key to the attic was at that very moment weighing down my dressing-gown pocket. He asked if he could come in and hunt around for his stuff; I hesitated, then said it was OK. I hadn't washed my hair for a week and I hadn't bothered to put my contacts in; I was wearing my glasses. I was too thin, because I wasn't eating enough, and my pink dressing gown was years old and grey from washing. I followed Julian around while he rummaged in the cupboard under the stairs, the utility room. The house was hot, because I'd had the central heating on for hours. Fuming to himself, he wondered what Hana had done with his things. He wasn't very interested in me.

The boy traipsed after us, complaining that he was bored. He wanted to watch TV, but Julian said that he watched too much of it and made him unpack some paper and pens from his backpack, then settled him down to draw at the kitchen table. I got the impression that the boy had been to Hana's house before. Julian was one of those parents whose attention to their children is inventive and forceful, inspiring – but I guessed that it might also be intermittent, abruptly withdrawn at any time, without explanation or with too much explanation. The child wasn't likeable: his white face was theatrically reproachful; he whined and never once smiled or thanked anyone for anything. Julian told me upstairs that the situation at home was tough. He was leaving his wife and moving out. The important thing was to make sure that the kids knew it didn't affect his love for them. That's why he was taking them camping.

— The weather's not very good for camping, I said.

He insisted that that was half the fun.

When I mentioned the locked attic room at the top of the house, he bounded up to rattle the door handle, frustrated that he couldn't get in.

— She didn't tell you where she keeps the key?

It would have been easy for me to produce it at this point, to explain that I'd noticed it in the tea-towel drawer, but for some reason I liked feeling its weight against my leg, holding something back from him. Finally, he decided to call Hana on her mobile. — She's still got her old number, right? He glanced at the clock to work out the time difference. I imagined Hana dishevelled and stale, roused from her sleep in Los Angeles.

— Hello, Hana, he said. — It's Julian. Yes, I know what time it is.

Walking away from me, he addressed himself with a fixed, strained smile into the phone. — Don't even start, he said in a subdued voice, intimately cruel and not meant for me to hear. — Don't even get started, Hana. I don't want to get started on all that all over again. I just want my camping gear.

After further urgent sotto voce exchanges, he covered the mouthpiece with his hand, gesturing to me. — She says to try in the knife-and-fork drawer.

— You've looked there, I said.

97

— Fuck, Hana. I'm taking my kids on a fucking holiday.

I went again into the kitchen, opening and closing a couple of drawers.

— Here it is, I said then. — Look, I've found it.

I went back into the room where he was telephoning, holding out the key on the palm of my hand. Julian didn't bother to explain to Hana, just cut off the call, snatched the key, and went running upstairs again to the attic, where he quickly found what he was looking for. I heard him humping stuff onto the landing, and the chink of metal tent poles in a bag. The boy was still absorbed in his drawing. When they'd gone, I noticed that he'd left it behind on the table: most of the page was blank, but a procession of tiny people was drawn neatly and precisely along the bottom – men, women and children, weaving their way among tall clumps of grass and jagged rocks.

I thought I'd never see Julian again, but that afternoon he called me on Hana's landline.

— Listen, he said. — What's your name? Listen, Laura. I told you I was moving out from home. Well, I need a place to store some boxes and it occurred to me that I could leave them at Hana's. She's got that attic for storage, so they won't be in your way – you won't even know they're there. It's just for the interim, while I find a place.

He said that Hana didn't mind, but I didn't really believe he had asked her.

— It'll all be gone, anyway, before she gets back from the States.

— I suppose I don't see why not, I said.

So he arranged to bring his boxes over around six. Something about his jubilant efficiency made me suspect that he was outmanoeuvring his wife, whisking his possessions out from under her nose before she could lay claim to anything. — I'll see you at six, Laura, he said.

When I put the phone down, I was frightened and excited, as if I had an assignation with a lover. This was preposterous, of course, and I knew it – I hadn't even liked the man and wasn't the least bit attracted to him. Also, he was only coming to drop off some boxes. Yet I hurried upstairs, burdened by the need to get ready for his arrival, as if it were momentous. It was only half past four – I had plenty of time. I washed my hair in the shower, with Hana's special revitalising shampoo, then I put on the thick towelling bathrobe that still smelled of her perfume. It was big on me, and I felt as if I were a little girl playing in my mother's clothes. Putting in my contacts, I studied my reflection, layering on foundation and then eyeshadow, mascara, lipstick; ordinarily, I didn't bother with any of this. The face that emerged in the mirror was recognisably mine – a wary small oval spoiled by a thin nose – but replete with new knowledge. Then I browsed through the blouses in Hana's wardrobe, looking for something to wear over my jeans; I chose a gauzy, sultry maroon top splotched with black flowers, cinched at the waist with a belt I'd found discarded in the attic – Middle Eastern, dark pink

99

embroidery, sewn with dangling silver coins. I wore a necklace of the silver coins, too. I pinned up my hair and sprayed on Hana's perfume.

When I was ready, I poured myself a glass of white wine from a bottle I'd put in the fridge. I had been careful with alcohol while I was living in Hana's house: I was afraid of getting drunk by myself every night. But this evening the first sips were delicious – a high green note like a bell at the front of my mind. I stood at an upstairs window watching the leaves blowing down from the trees onto the wet black tarmac. After a while, Julian was late, and I'd finished the glass of wine. Just as I'd decided with relief that he wasn't coming after all, he turned up in a white camper van, parking where there was a space across the road. He rang the bell and I buzzed him in, then went down to the front door, where several boxes were already stacked on the doorstep; Julian was across the road, unpacking more boxes from the van. There were a lot more boxes than he had suggested on the phone – and not only boxes but other stuff: bedding and an anglepoise lamp and a couple of racing bikes.

He explained that he was late because things had been more complicated than he'd anticipated. — Where's that key? I'll just pop these up in the attic, then I'll clear out of your way. They'll honestly only be here for a week or two.

— Are you leaving your wife to be with Hana? I asked.

He barked with disbelieving laughter.

— You're kidding. Who gave you that idea? Don't tell me she did.

— No one. I just wondered.

— No fear of that, he said. — Hana's not really my type.

I gave him the key and waited in the kitchen while he ran up and down the stairs, taking them two at a time, carrying up his stuff; he was muscular, as if he went to the gym or took regular exercise. I could hear that he had to move things around in the attic to get it all inside. By the time he came looking for me to return the key, he was breathing hard, and there were dark patches of sweat on his T-shirt. He picked up the jacket he'd slung over the back of a chair.

— Would you like a glass of wine? I asked, as I had planned.

— Better not, I'm driving.

— Cup of tea?

I think he was surprised that I persisted. Noticing something, he took a step towards me, reaching for my necklace of coins and fingering it. — I remember this. Isn't it Hana's?

— She gave it to me, I lied.

For the first time then, I saw him take me in: distinctly, as if an image of me flickered across his expression and was swallowed inside. He held on for a moment to the necklace connecting us, then let it drop so that it struck me on the breastbone. I wondered if he recognised the blouse, too.

— Well, why not? he said. — A glass of wine.

We sat at the counter where Hana and I had sat to make arrangements. Julian glowed with the satisfaction of having accomplished his pre-emptive strike against his wife. With the boxes stowed, there was time now to focus the strong beam of his attention on me. I felt its heat and knew that he was seeing at last how different I looked.

— So, Laura. What are you doing here in Hana-land?

Disguised, I was able to perform a part: I could hear myself sounding carefree and flirtatious. I explained that I hardly knew Hana and was staying in her house because, like him, I was escaping my marriage.

He raised his glass. — To marriage, and all those who abandon ship.

— To abandoning ship, I said.

He asked me about my husband, and I exaggerated how dull he was; I made it sound as if I were the one who'd fallen out of love. Julian had a lot of ideas about relationships and their natural sell-by dates (that was his phrase). — If the thing's dead, he said, — then the kindest thing to do is walk away from it. You're only prolonging the agony otherwise.

I thought he might be the sort of man who heard himself expounding his own ideas inside his head even when he was alone – reasonably, persuasively. Meanwhile, I began to feel peculiar as I drank my way through my second glass of wine. I remembered that I hadn't eaten anything since breakfast; then, when I tried to step down from the high stool at the counter, my foot tangled in the crossbar and I staggered and almost fell. Julian was immediately proficient, practical. Supporting me, he steered me to an armchair.

— What's the matter? Are you going to throw up? What have you taken?

I explained that I hadn't taken anything. And then I told him the whole story – how I'd run out of money and hadn't begun looking for a job yet, and how over the weeks I'd eaten everything in Hana's freezer and now it was empty.

— You're actually fainting from hunger?

— I'm definitely going shopping tomorrow. It was just silly, having that second glass of wine.

Something about my situation touched him and made him laugh – I think he rather liked imagining me as a starving waif. He rummaged through the kitchen cupboards looking for something I could eat, but I'd gone through those cupboards weeks before. Then he stood frowning, as if I were a puzzle, half intriguing and half bothersome. — Well, Laura. It looks as if I might owe you a supper. I suppose you did me a favour. I'll drive up to the deli. What do you like?

— Oh, anything, I said, trying to remember the freezer. — Chicken Maryland, chicken Kiev, shrimp in teriyaki sauce . . .

— Not that frozen shit Hana eats. I'm going to cook real food.

I saw that his seduction, if it came, would be like this – not heartfelt and hesitant but brisk and with an element of firm corrective. I was ready to submit to it.

He tucked a rug over me before he left, put a glass of water within reach, and tested my forehead competently with his palm.

While he was out, the telephone rang and I answered it from the armchair.

— So what happened? Hana said. — Did he find his bloody tent?

— Who? Oh, Julian. Yes, it was in the attic.

— What kind of mood was he in? Did he say anything about me?

— Not really, I said. — Who is he?

— He's a bit of a nightmare, actually. He and I had a thing going at some point. Luckily I bailed out pretty quickly.

— What does he do?

— Oh, some sort of Web design. He talks up the charity work, but it's mostly corporate.

I told her then that he was cooking me supper. For a bruised, long moment, she was soundless at the other end of the line. — He's still there? Julian's there in the house?

— He's just taken the van up to the deli, to buy what he needs.

— He's cooking you supper? I thought he came for his tent?

— He came back again this evening.

I didn't mention the boxes.

— I can't get my head around this. Do you two know each other?

— It's just a friendly thing, because I helped him with the key. I was hungry, so he offered to cook.

Hana took this in. — I see, she said in a voice so remote that it reminded me how far away Los Angeles actually was. — It's weird, because he used to make such an issue out of being home for mealtimes with his kids.

I didn't try to explain that he was leaving his wife.

— Oh, well, she said. — Enjoy. I hope he makes you something nice.

Julian brought back muesli and fruit and poppy-seed cake, as well as the ingredients for supper. Cutting a chunk of bread, he told me to eat that to start with, and to drink plenty of water. There was a lot of sizzling and show and split-second timing as he cooked, and even a high leap of naked flame when he burned off the alcohol from his sauce. He complained that it was characteristic for Hana's kitchen to be full of expensive equipment although she lived on takeaways; he told me that he only ate organic food, that he cycled fifty miles every weekend, and that he'd designed and built himself a loft studio in the house he was leaving, but didn't begrudge the loss of it because he was always moving on and looking forward.

I'd never have picked Julian out as a sensuous type if I hadn't read Hana's diary; he seemed too busy and prosaic, without the abstracted dreamy edges I'd always imagined in people who gave themselves over to their erotic lives. And yet, because of the secret things I knew about him, I was fixated on him the whole time I watched him cook, and then afterwards, while we sat opposite each other eating at the little table he pulled up to my armchair. I told myself that if he left without anything happening, then I had lost my chance and I would die. I wasn't melting or longing for him to touch me or anything like that; the desire wasn't in my body but wedged in my mind, persistent and burrowing. I didn't even like Julian much. But liking people and even loving them seemed to me now like ways of keeping yourself safe, and I didn't want to be safe. I wanted to cross the threshold and be initiated into real life. My innocence was a sign of something maimed or unfinished in me.

The food was delicious – couscous with a sauce made from peppers and pine nuts and mushrooms and pancetta. It would be good for me, Julian said, because it wasn't too rich. He told me to eat slowly, and he finished first, wiping his mouth and sitting back in his chair to observe me.

— It's great to watch someone enjoying their food, he said.

— Better than the chicken Kiev.

— I should say so.

I was uncomfortable under his scrutiny but gave myself up to it, hoping that I wasn't dropping couscous everywhere.

— I can't quite make you out, Laura, he said. — I'm curious about you. You were as hostile as a little fox when I came for the tent this morning.

— I'm not really a morning person.

— Yet this evening I got the feeling you wanted me to stay – and not only because you were in need of a square meal.

I bent my hot face over my wine glass. — I've been spending a lot of time alone.

— Solitude's like a drug, he said. — You use it. You can't let it use you.

(Really? I heard my husband querying in my mind – contemptuously, witheringly. Is it actually anything like a drug? I don't think so.)

Julian leaned forward and put his hand on my jeans above my knee, spreading his fingers and bearing down with an unambiguous pressure. Then I felt all the bodily part of desire kick into life all right – the melting and the thrumming and the longing. So this is how it begins, I thought: the passage over into the other place. Very carefully, readying myself, I put my glass down on the table. But just at that moment the phone rang and he pulled his hand away.

It was Hana again. — Is Julian still there? she asked urgently, secretively.

— He is, I said.

I took the phone and walked away with my back to him, into the next room.

— Well, listen. I've been calling around a few friends. You should be careful. Apparently, he's splitting up with Suzanne. So watch out for him. Julian's a snake. He'll take advantage of you because you're vulnerable. I know he will. I should think he's sniffing out somewhere to sleep for a few days.

— I'm not vulnerable, I said. — Don't worry about me.

She was exasperated by my tone. — I'm pretty miffed, actually, by the idea of him making himself at home in my house while I'm away. You'd understand if you knew the half of what's gone on.

— I'm sorry. I thought he was a friend of yours. But don't worry, anyway – we've almost finished supper.

— And then he's going?

I said I could hardly push him out into the street the moment we'd cleared our plates. — I owe him a coffee, at least.

— He doesn't drink coffee, she said gloomily.

She rang off, and I returned to the kitchen. Julian was standing with his back to the window, hands in his pockets, wearing the jacket he'd taken off to cook. I knew at once that something had changed during my absence.

— Was that Hana looking after you? he said, amused.

— I don't need looking after.

— Couldn't you cheerfully strangle her sometimes?

— You don't have to hurry away, I said. — Won't you stay for some tea? Is this because Hana called?

Julian was suffused with regret, positively rosy with his own sheer decency in turning me down. — You're feeling better now, aren't you?

— Don't go, I cried.

I seized him by the sleeves of his jacket, so that there could be no mistake about what I was offering; up close, I was submerged in his heat and the dense miasma of his smells, frying and sweat, intoxicating in the madness of

the moment. Kindly, patiently, he disengaged himself. —
It's got nothing to do with Hana, he said. — I have to
be somewhere else. Somebody will be wondering where
I am. Don't forget we're going camping in the morning.

I pressed the front door shut behind him and then, for a
long moment, while I rested my fingertips with finality on
the cherry-red paint inside, I didn't know whether I was
going to die or not. I waited there, head bowed, for the
wave to break over me – this was it, the whole humiliation.
I was so exposed that I might as well have been skinned
and turned inside out. Then my eyes fastened on two
protruding screws, one on each side of the interior of Hana's
letter box: in their functional ugliness they were reassuring.
I lifted my head and looked on tiptoe through the security
peephole. Julian was gone; shooting the bolt across, I was
alone. My thoughts wheeled around and down and then
struck bottom: not, to my surprise, on despair but on
something else after all – hard, bleak, grey, satisfactory
freedom. Letting go of the strain of yearning was a relief,
like stretched elastic retracting. When I walked into the
kitchen, I saw that Julian had left a fifty-pound note tucked
under the pepper pot. Working tenderly and cautiously
around my self-esteem, as if it were convalescent, I cleared
up – stacked most of the dishes and pans in the machine,
rinsed a few delicate things, wiped down the surfaces and
the cooker and the table, put the leftover food in the fridge.
 I thought I might watch a film – one of the art films
that Hana had left downstairs for me. In the bedroom I
changed back into my pyjamas and dressing gown, and

109

on impulse hunted out my box of souvenirs – the perfume bottle, a few postcards, the pebbles. I had picked up these pebbles from a favourite beach I visited with my parents when I was a teenager: a fierce sea in a rocky cleft at the bottom of a steep descent through gorse bushes. One of them fitted snugly in my hand, and I hung on to it all the way through Pasolini's *Theorem*, which I had seen before and which meant a lot to me. Washed smooth, the pebble was reddish brown, speckled with blue and cream like a bird's egg, consoling.

Julian must have taken the attic key with him, because the next day I couldn't find it anywhere. Hana was annoyed when she got back from LA and had to get a locksmith in to open the door; she didn't mention finding Julian's stuff stowed away in there, so I assumed he'd collected it sometime when I was out – he must have had a front-door key left over from the days of their affair. I had begun to be out most of the time, because the very next day after our supper I started looking for a job – and then I found one, working as a receptionist for a publisher of medical and scientific journals. Eventually I found a room too, in a shared house with some old friends. The funny thing was that after my evening with Julian I knew I came across as older and more experienced. People seemed to take me more seriously – as if I'd been initiated into something after all, although nothing had happened. I don't think Hana ever believed that nothing had happened. She came to see me at my new place one evening, looking striking in a belted mac, with dark red lipstick and a beret pinned on her hair at a dramatic angle.

— I need to know about Julian, she said.

In good faith, I wanted to be guileless, transparent to her. I confessed about his storing the boxes and taking them away again – though I couldn't bring myself to mention reading her diary.

— And that's all?

I tried to clear my face, but something must have showed there which she couldn't penetrate. She kept her eyes on me, and her watchfulness had respect and even fear in it, as if I were the one with secrets.

Bad Dreams

A child woke up in the dark. She seemed to swim up into consciousness as if to a surface which she then broke through, looking around with her eyes open. At first the darkness was implacable. She might have arrived anywhere: all that was certain was her own self, lying on her side, her salty smell and her warmth, her knees pulled up to her skinny chest inside the cocoon of her brushed-nylon nightdress. But as she stared into the darkness familiar forms began to loom through it: the pale outline of a window, printed by the street lamp against the curtains; the horizontals on the opposite wall, which were the shelves where she and her brother kept their books and toys. Beside the window she could make out a rectangle of wool cloth tacked up; her mother had appliquéd onto it a sleigh and two horses and a driver cracking his whip, first gluing on the pieces and then outlining them with machine stitching – star shapes in blue thread for the falling snowflakes, lines of red stitching for the reins and the twisting whip. The child knew all these details by heart, though she couldn't see them in the dark. She was where she always was when she woke up: in her own bedroom, in the top bunk, her younger brother asleep in the lower one.

Her mother and father were in bed and asleep, too. The basement flat was small enough that, if they were awake, she would have heard the sewing machine or the wireless, or her father practising the trumpet or playing jazz records. She struggled to sit up out of the tightly wound nest of sheets and blankets; she was asthmatic and feared not being able to catch her breath. Cold night air struck her shoulders. It was strange to stare into the room with wide-open eyes and feel the darkness yielding only the smallest bit, as if it were pressing back against her efforts to penetrate it. Something had happened, she was sure, while she was asleep. She didn't know what it was at first, but the strong dread it had left behind didn't subside with the confusion of waking. Then she remembered that this thing had happened inside her sleep, in her dream. She had dreamed something horrible, and so plausible that it was vividly present as soon as she remembered it.

She had dreamed that she was reading her favourite book, the one she read over and over and actually had been reading earlier that night, until her mother came to turn off the light. In fact, she could feel the book's hard corner pressing into her leg now through the blankets. In the dream, she had been turning its pages as usual when, beyond the story's familiar last words, she discovered an extra section that she had never seen before, a short paragraph set on a page by itself, headed 'Epilogue'. She was an advanced reader for nine and knew about prologues and epilogues – though it didn't occur to her then that she was the author of her own dreams and must have invented this epilogue herself. It seemed so completely a found thing, alien and unanticipated, coming from outside herself, against her will.

In the real book she loved, *Swallows and Amazons*, six children spent their summers in perfect freedom, sailing dinghies on a lake, absorbed in adventures and rivalries that were half invented games and half truth, pushing across the threshold of safety into a thrilling unknown. All the details in the book had the solidity of life, though it wasn't her own life – she didn't have servants or boats or a lake or an absent father in the navy. She had read all the other books in the series, too, and she acted out their stories with her friends at school, although they lived in a city and none of them had ever been sailing. The world of *Swallows and Amazons* existed in a dimension parallel to their own, touching it only in their games. They had a *Swallows and Amazons* club, and took turns bringing in 'grub' to eat, 'grog' and 'pemmican'; they sewed badges, and wrote notes in secret code. All of them wanted to be Nancy Blackett, the strutting pirate girl, though they would settle for Titty Walker, sensitive and watchful.

Now the child seemed to see the impersonal print of the dream epilogue, written on the darkness in front of her eyes. *John and Roger both went on to*, it began, in a businesslike voice. Of course, the words weren't actually in front of her eyes, and parts of what was written were elusive when she sought them; certain sentences, though, were scored into her awareness as sharply as if she'd heard them read aloud. *Roger drowned at sea in his twenties.* Roger was the youngest of them all, the ship's boy, in whom she had only ever been mildly interested: this threw him into a terrible new prominence. *John suffered with a bad heart. The Blackett sisters . . . long illnesses. Titty, killed in an unfortunate accident.* The litany of deaths tore jaggedly into the tissue that the book had woven, making everything lopsided and hideous. The epilogue's gloating bland language, complacently regretful, seemed to relish catching her out in her dismay. Oh, didn't you know? *Susan lived to a ripe old age.* Susan was the dullest of the Swallows, tame and sensible, in charge of cooking and housekeeping. Still, the idea of her 'ripe old age' was full of horror: wasn't she just a girl, with everything ahead of her?

The child knew that the epilogue existed only in her dream, but she couldn't dispel the taint of it, clinging to her thoughts. When she was younger she had called to her mother if she woke in the night, but something stopped her from calling out now: she didn't want to tell anyone about this. Once the words were said aloud, she would never be rid of them; it was better to keep them hidden. And she was afraid, anyway, that her mother wouldn't understand the awfulness of the dream if she tried to explain it: she might laugh or think it was silly. For the first time, the child felt as if she were alone in her own home – its rooms spread out about her, invisible in the night, seemed unlike their usual selves. The book touching her leg through the blankets frightened her, and she thought she might never be able to open it again. Not wanting to lie down in the place where she'd had the dream, she swung over the side rail of the bed and reached with her bare feet for the steps of the ladder – the lower bunk was a cave so dark that she couldn't make out the shape of her sleeping brother. Then she felt the carpet's gritty wool under her toes.

The children's bedroom, the bathroom, papered in big blue roses, and their parents' room were all at the front of the massive Victorian house, which was four storeys tall, including this basement flat; sometimes the child was aware of the other flats above theirs, full of the furniture of other lives, pressing down on their heads. Quietly she opened her bedroom door. The doors to the kitchen and the lounge, which were at the back of the flat, stood open onto the windowless hallway; a thin blue light, falling through them, lay in rectangles on the hall carpet. She had read about moonlight, but had never taken in its reality before: it made the lampshade of Spanish wrought iron, which had always hung from a chain in the hallway, seem suddenly as barbaric as a cage or a portcullis in a castle.

Everything was tidy in the kitchen: the dishcloth had been wrung out and hung on the edge of the plastic washing-up bowl; something on a plate was wrapped in greaseproof paper; the sewing machine was put away under its cover at one end of the table. The pieces of Liberty lawn print, which her mother was cutting out for one of her ladies, were folded carefully in their paper bag to keep them clean. Liberty lawn: her mother named it reverently, like an incantation – though the daily business of her sewing wasn't reverent but briskly pragmatic, cutting and pinning and snipping at seams with pinking shears, running the machine with her head bent close to the work in bursts of concentration, one hand always raised to the wheel to slow it, or breaking threads quickly in the little clip behind the needle. The chatter of the sewing machine, racing and easing and halting and starting up again, was like a busy engine driving their days. There were always threads and pins scattered on the floor around where her mother was working – you had to be careful where you stepped.

In the lounge, the child paddled her toes in the hair of the white goatskin rug. Gleaming, uncanny, half reverted to its animal past, the rug yearned to the moon, which was balanced on top of the wall at the back of the paved yard. The silver frame of her parents' wedding photograph and the yellow brass of her father's trumpet – in its case with the lid open, beside the music stand – shone with the same pale light. Lifting the heavy lid of the gramophone, she breathed in the forbidden smell of the records nestled in their felt-lined compartments, then touched the pages heaped on her father's desk: his meaning, densely tangled in his black italic writing, seemed more accessible through her fingertips in the dark than it ever was in daylight, when its difficulty thwarted her. He was studying for his degree in the evenings, after teaching at school all day. She and her brother played

118

quietly so as not to disturb him; their mother had impressed upon them the importance of his work. He was writing about a book, *Leviathan*: his ink bottle had left imprints on the desk's leather inlay, and he stored his notes on a shelf in cardboard folders, carefully labelled – the pile of folders growing ever higher. The child was struck by the melancholy of this accumulation: sometimes she felt a pang of fear for her father, as if he were exposed and vulnerable – and yet when he wasn't working he charmed her with his jokes, pretending to be poisoned when he tasted the cakes she had made, teasing her school friends until they blushed. She never feared in the same way for her mother: her mother was capable; she was the whole world.

In their absence, her parents were more distinctly present to her than usual, as individuals with their own unfathomable adult preoccupations. She was aware of their lives running backwards from this moment, into a past that she could never enter. This moment, too, the one fitted around her now as inevitably and closely as a skin, would one day become the past: its details then would seem remarkable and poignant, and she would never be able to return inside them. The chairs in the lounge, formidable in the dimness, seemed drawn up as if for a spectacle, waiting more attentively than if they were filled with people: the angular recliner built of black tubular steel, with lozenges of polished wood for arms; the cone-shaped wicker basket in its round wrought-iron frame; the black-painted wooden armchair with orange cushions; and the low divan covered in striped olive-green cotton. The reality of the things in the room seemed more substantial to the child than she was herself – and she wanted in a sudden passion to break something, to disrupt this world of her home, sealed in its mysterious stillness, where her bare feet made no sound on the lino or the carpets.

On impulse, using all her strength, she pushed at the recliner from behind, tipping it over slowly until it was upside down, with its top resting on the carpet and its legs in the air, the rubber ferrules on its feet unexpectedly silly in the moonlight, like prim, tiny shoes. Then she tipped over the painted chair, so that its cushions flopped out. She pulled the wicker cone out of its frame and turned the frame over, flipped up the goatskin rug. She managed to make very little noise, just a few soft bumps and thuds; when she had finished, though, the room looked as if a hurricane had blown through it, throwing the chairs about. She was shocked by what she'd effected, but gratified, too: the after-sensation of strenuous work tingled in her legs and arms, and she was breathing fast; her whole body rejoiced in the chaos. Perhaps it would be funny when her parents saw it in the morning. At any rate, nothing – nothing – would ever make her tell them that she'd done it. They would never know, and that was funny, too. A private hilarity bubbled up in her, though she wouldn't give way to it; she didn't want to make a sound. And at that very moment, as she surveyed her crazy handiwork, the moon sank below the top of the wall outside and the room darkened, all its solidity withdrawn.

*   *   *

The child's mother woke up early, in the dawn. Had her little boy called out to her? Sometimes in the night he had strange fits of crying, during which he didn't recognise her and screamed in her arms for his mummy. She listened, but heard nothing – yet she was as fully, promptly awake as if there had been some summons or a bell had rung. Carefully she sat up, not wanting to wake her sleeping husband, who was lying on his side, with his knees drawn up and his back to her, the bristle of his crew cut the only part of him visible above the blankets. The room was just as she had left it when she went to sleep, except that his clothes were thrown on top of hers on the chair; he had stayed up late, working on his essay. She remembered dimly that when he got into bed she had turned over, snuggling up to him, and that in her dream she had seemed to fit against the shape of him as sweetly as a nut into its shell, losing herself inside him. But now he was lost, somewhere she couldn't follow him. Sometimes in the mornings, especially if they hadn't made love the night before, she would wake to find herself beside this stranger, buried away from her miles deep, frowning in his sleep. His immobility then seemed a kind of comment, or a punishment, directed at her.

The grey light in the room was diffuse and hesitant. Even on sunny days, these rooms at the front of the flat weren't bright. She had been happy in this flat at first, in the new freedom of her married life, but now she resented the neighbours always brooding overhead and was impatient to move to a place they could have all to themselves. But that would have to wait until he finished his degree. She eased out from under the warmth of the blankets. Now that she was thoroughly awake she needed to pee before she tried to sleep again. As she got out of bed, her reflection stood up indefatigably to meet her in the gilt-framed mirror that was one of her junk-shop finds, mounted in an alcove beside the window, with a trailing philodendron trained around it. The phantom in the baby-doll nightdress was enough like Monica Vitti (everyone said she looked like Monica Vitti) to make her straighten her back in self-respect; and she was aware of yesterday's L'Air du Temps in the sleepy heat of her skin.

In the hall, she listened at the door of the children's room, which stood ajar – nothing. The lavatory was chilly: its tiny high window made it feel like a prison cell, but a blackbird sang liquidly outside in the yard. On the way back to bed, she looked into the kitchen, where everything was as she'd left it – he hadn't even made his cocoa or eaten the sandwich she'd put out for him before he came to bed. His refraining made her tense her jaw, as if he had repudiated her and preferred his work. She should have been a painter, she thought in a flash of anger, not a housewife and a dressmaker. But at art college she'd been overawed by the fine arts students, who were mostly experienced grown men, newly returned from doing their national service in India and Malaya. Still, her orderly kitchen reassured her: the scene of her daily activity, poised and quiescent now, awaiting the morning, when she'd pick it up again with renewed energy. Perhaps he'd like bacon for his breakfast – she had saved up her housekeeping to buy him some. His mother had cooked bacon for him every morning.

When she glanced into the lounge, her shock at the sight of the chairs thrown about was as extreme as a hand clapped over her mouth from behind. The violence was worse because it was frozen in silence – had lain in wait, gloating, while she suspected nothing. Someone had broken in. She was too afraid in the first moments to call out to her husband. She waited in the doorway, holding her breath, for the movement that would give the intruder away; it was awful to think that a few minutes ago she had gone unprotected all the way down the lonely passageway to the lavatory. Then, as her panic subsided, she took in the odd specificity of the chaos. Only the chairs were overturned, at the centre of the room; nothing else had been touched, nothing pulled off the shelves and thrown on the floor, nothing smashed. The lounge windows were tightly closed – just as the back door had surely been closed in the kitchen. Nothing had been taken. Had it? The wireless was intact on its shelf. Rousing out of her stupor, she crossed to the desk and opened the drawer where her husband kept his band earnings. The money was safe: three pound ten in notes and some loose change, along with his pipe and pipe cleaners and dirty tobacco pouch, the smell of which stayed on her fingers when she closed the drawer.

Instead of waking her husband, she tried the window catches, then went around checking the other rooms of the flat. The kitchen door and the front door were both securely bolted, and no one could have climbed in through the tiny window in the lavatory. Soundless on her bare feet, she entered the children's bedroom and stood listening to their breathing. Her little boy stirred in his sleep but didn't cry; her daughter was spread-eagled awkwardly amid the menagerie of her stuffed toys and dolls. Their window, too, was fastened shut. There was no intruder in the flat, and only one explanation for the crazy scene in the front room: her imagination danced with affront and dismay. Chilled, she returned to stand staring in the lounge. Her husband was moody, and she'd always known that he had anger buried in him. But he'd never done anything like this before – nothing so naked and outrageous. She supposed he must have got frustrated with his studies before he came to bed. Or was the disorder a derisory message meant for her, because he despised her homemaking, her domesti-cation of the free life he'd once had? Perhaps the mess was even supposed to be some kind of brutal joke. She couldn't imagine how she had slept through the outburst.

This time, for once, she was clearly in the right, wasn't she? He had been childish, giving way to his frustration – as if she didn't feel fed up sometimes. And he criticised her for her bad temper! He had such high standards for everyone else! From now on, she would hold on to this new insight into him, no matter how reasonable he seemed. Her disdain hurt her, like a bruise to the chest; she was more used to admiring him. But it was also exhilarating: she seemed to see the future with great clarity, looking forward through a long tunnel of antagonism, in which her husband was her enemy. This awful truth appeared to be something she had always known, though in the past it had been clouded in uncertainty and now she saw it starkly. Calmly and quietly she picked up each chair, put back the cushions which had tumbled onto the carpet, straightened the goatskin rug. The room looked as serene as if nothing had ever happened in it. The joke of its serenity erupted inside her like bubbles of soundless laughter. Nothing – nothing – would ever make her acknowledge what he'd done, or the message he'd left for her, although when he saw the room restored to its rightful order, he would know that she knew. She would wait for him to be the first to acknowledge in words the passage of this silent violence between them.

In the bedroom, she lay down beside her husband with her back turned; her awareness of her situation seemed pure and brilliant, and she expected to lie awake, burning at his nearness. There was less than an hour to wait before she had to get up again; she'd got back into bed only because her feet were cold and it was too early to switch on the electric fire in the kitchen. But almost at once she dropped into a deep sleep – particularly blissful, as if she were falling down through syrupy darkness, her limbs unbound and bathing in warmth. When she woke again – this time her little boy really was calling out to her – she remembered immediately what had happened in the night, but she also felt refreshed and blessed.

A young wife fried bacon for her husband: the smell of it filled the flat. Her son was eating cereal at the table.

Her husband was preoccupied, packing exercise books into his worn briefcase, opening the drawer in his desk where he kept his pipe and tobacco, dropping these into the pocket of his tweed jacket. But he came at some point to stand behind his wife at the stove and put his arms around her, nuzzling her neck, kissing her behind her ear, and she leaned back into his kiss, as she always did, tilting her head to give herself to him.

When the bacon was ready, she served it up on a plate with fried bread and a tomato and poured his tea, then went to find out why their daughter was dawdling in the bedroom. The girl was sitting on the edge of her brother's bunk, trying to pull on her knee-length socks with one hand while she held a book open in front of her eyes with the other. Her thin freckled face was nothing like her mother's. One white sock was twisted around her leg with its dirty heel sticking out at the front, and the book was surely the same one she had already read several times. The child was insistent, though, that she needed to start reading it all over again, from the beginning. Her mother took the book away and chivvied her along.

Flight

Claire had to fly over from Philadelphia to the UK for a business meeting. The night before the night she flew, she made a stupid mistake, drank too much and went to bed with a man she didn't know very well, didn't even like all that much. Her plane left at six the following evening, flying away from the setting sun. The alcohol was still toxic in her system, she wasn't a great drinker and wasn't used to it, hadn't done anything stupid like that for a while. She didn't want to eat anything and could only drink tonic water. When she took the fizzing glass she saw that her hand shook, and felt humiliated though no one else could have noticed. One of the flight attendants in business class, an Englishwoman with an eager, bony face, too elaborately made up, probably in her early forties – Claire's own age – wanted to make a fuss of her, admiring her coat, gushing over her handbag while she stowed it for her in the overhead locker. She offered up that comedy of a greed for material things, designer goods, which was a currency between women. But Claire wasn't in the mood for female solidarity, she cut her short and the attendant treated her after that with careful respect, no hint of resentment. Even this little display of her own power struck Claire bitterly, like a foretaste of England. If ever she was stand-offish at work her American colleagues held it against her, putting it down to British snootiness, probably believing she came from the British privileged classes.

After they'd served the meal, which she refused, the flight attendants tried to get everyone asleep for the short, false night. As the talk ceased and silence fell, they were all more aware of the plane forging forwards with such force, shuddering with the violence of its effort. Bodies were shrouded in their pale cotton quilts. A few passengers were reading, in cones of subdued light from overhead or the ghost-light from laptops or tablets. Claire could have been going through the background material on her new clients, but the thought of the dullness of those files stirred up traces of nausea, like silt in a pond. She could still feel the lovemaking in her body, not in a pleasant way but as a bruised, raw fatigue, as if her skin had been ground against her bones. As the time passed more detail came back to her, but she didn't get used to what she'd done, it seemed more inexplicable and disastrously mistaken. Luckily she had put aside a whole day in London for shopping or sight-seeing, before she began her meetings. As soon as she got to her hotel in the morning, she could run a hot bath, then block out the light and sleep, hibernating

while the last toxins leached out of her. Her whole existence seemed only aimed at those hours ahead, of oblivion
and privacy.

Waking in her hotel room in the afternoon, she felt
much better. Bright light was pricking round the edges
of the heavy curtains, and when she first opened her
eyes she thought that there must be brilliant sunshine
outside, a perfect day – though in fact the sun wasn't
shining, the city was only suffused in its familiar soft
autumn light, pink and pearly grey. Even through the
sealed windows the muffled noise of the perpetual traffic
reached her, a clangour of building sites, the chiming
of steel against steel. Her room was on the seventh
floor, with a view of a busy small park and trees down
below – she had chosen a hotel near Liverpool Street
Station because she needed to be in Chingford first
thing in the morning. She showered again, then put on
some of the clean clothes she had unpacked before she
collapsed into bed, did her face quickly and skilfully at
the dressing table. You had to dress right down in
London, the classic good taste which worked in America
looked dated here.

  She had made up her mind about something while
she slept. Her niece Amy, her sister Susan's daughter,
had a new baby and she ought to see it. This wasn't
straightforward because Claire and Susan had quarrelled, they hadn't spoken for several years. This quarrel
shadowed all Claire's relations with her family at
home: it was time now to dispel the shadows. She had

to spend all day tomorrow in Chingford, and on Wednesday and Thursday she would be running training sessions in Northampton, for the technicians in the UK service office of the American company she worked for. But her return flight wasn't till Saturday and when she was free on Thursday evening she would catch a train north, go home and surprise them. She didn't let herself think beyond this initial impulse, knowing how easy it would be to talk herself out of going. She'd made approaches to Susan before and been rebuffed; any efforts at reconciliation had always come from her side.

Instead she went out in search of presents for the baby – a boy, Calum. She always liked her first hours in England, slipping in unnoticed in the crowd, at home in her own tribe, submerged among the English voices, southern ones and northern ones – and the foreign voices which were part of it. As the autumn day thickened into dusky evening, the white light from the shop windows seemed more seductive – the lovely things laid out so subtly, not blatantly, to tempt you inside. There was so much money in London now, everything was glossy with money and expensive taste. Streets had been pedestrianised and planted with young trees, their twiggy silhouettes strung with more white lights; a busker was playing classical music on the violin. The shoppers dawdled purposefully, with a subdued excitement. Eventually Claire chose a shawl for the baby, in very fine cream wool, as light as cobwebs: it cost a fortune but she couldn't resist it, enjoyed watching the girl wrap it so deftly in tissue paper, securing it with pretty stickers, tying it with blue ribbon.

She bought perfume for Amy and a T-shirt for Ben, Amy's boyfriend, the baby's father – whom Claire hadn't met. She remembered to buy a T-shirt for Ryan too, Susan's youngest, who was still at home: they were all of them living piled in together somehow, in the old three-bedroomed terrace house where Claire and Susan had grown up. Then Claire spent a long time looking for a silk scarf for Susan, picking up one after another, wondering about colours, testing the liquid fall of silk against her hand – as if this choice were the problem, rather than anything between them in the past. In the end she went for a very full square in a tan and leaf-green paisley pattern, slightly retro – this would surely look nice in Leeds as well as in London. For herself she bought a little false fur tippet backed in yellow satin; it was colder here than in Philadelphia, and the tippet had just the touch of stylish irony she'd been in search of. Her face was piquant, framed in the soft fur in the shop mirror. She wasn't too bad for her age – petite, very thin, very fine-boned, with a sharp nose and good jawline, deep-set hooded grey eyes. But she looked quickly away from her reflection, remembering the other night.

Claire didn't call or text to let anyone know she was coming. She'd finished in Northampton by lunchtime on Thursday and arrived in Leeds around five, when it was beginning to get dark. Tactfully she left her suitcase at the station, and all she brought with her in the taxi was the carrier full of presents, as well as a few overnight things and a change of clothes in a shoulder bag, in case she was invited to stay. She told the driver to drop her at the end of her old street, which stretched out of sight in the gloom under the street lights; this was one of a succession of red-brick Victorian working-class terraces running roughly parallel to one another, all built in a hurry at the end of the nineteenth century. There were no trees or front gardens and the front doors opened directly onto the pavement; the only variety was in the different colours of the doors, or if some house-fronts were rendered or pebble-dashed. The street was empty and Claire's footsteps sounded eerily loud, the click-clack of her heels bouncing off the brick fronts. Uneasily she felt as though this moment of approaching her home could belong to any time in the past, it was so saturated with familiarity and the place was so unaltered – she might be coming home from school, or visiting from London when her parents were still alive.

But the present flooded back, as soon as Amy opened the front door to her. Behind the street's facade, each house was its own burst of noise and colour, done up or not done up in its own style: the woodchip paper in Claire's old hall had been painted over with a shocking pink – that was probably Amy's idea, not Susan's. Nothing was the same. Unfamiliar coats were laden on unfamiliar coat hooks, the narrow hallway was almost impassable with heaps of trainers and shoes and a buggy. A television was on in the back room; Amy was yelling something over her shoulder, then she turned to peer out doubtfully into the dusk. It was years since she had seen her aunt in person, though they were often in contact on Facebook or by Skype – anyway, Claire was supposed to be in America. — Auntie Claire! Is that you? What are you doing here?

She sounded hostile, but Claire knew not to read too much into it. Submerging in the voices and manner from her old home – so wary and flattening and grudging – was always a shock at first, before she got used to it again. That old way of being gripped her with mingled nostalgia and dread. — I've come to see the baby, haven't I? Can I come in? Is Susan here?

— She's not back from work yet. I thought it was her when the bell went.

Claire knew from the pictures on Facebook that Amy had put on a lot of weight in her pregnancy, but she still had her sulky, sexy prettiness. Her blonde hair, dark at the roots, was scraped back tightly in a scrunchy and yesterday's make-up was sooty under her eyes; there was a silver ring in her nose. She was wearing stretch tracksuit bottoms and socks, and under her T-shirt her breasts were swollen and shapeless.

— I've brought a bottle of bubbly, I thought we could wet the baby's head.

— The baby's driving me nuts, Auntie Claire. He's a nightmare, he doesn't sleep. You can keep him if you like. Take him back to America with you.

Following Amy down the hallway and into the back room, Claire thought she could smell that sweat of new motherhood she'd smelled on other women before – not quite unpleasant, milky and salty and frowsty. In spite of Amy's complaining, she actually seemed complacent in her slouchy, sloppy physical collapse – as if the baby had solved some problem about who she ought to be. Claire had last seen her niece when she was sixteen, mouthy and edgy and sprightly, very clever at school; then Susan had been so disappointed when she wouldn't try for university. Instead she'd ended up working in Topshop – and now this.

The back room was hot, and entirely taken over by baby things: a Moses basket and a plastic changing mat and packs of disposable nappies, a bag full of changing kit, blankets and muslin cloths draped everywhere, a clothes dryer laden with baby clothes, one of those low-slung bouncy chairs. A big good-looking boy with dyed fair hair sprawled on the sofa, watching *Family Guy* on the huge television set, laughing loudly at it: this must be Ben. He too was wearing tracksuit bottoms and thick woolly slipper-socks – and no doubt the tomcat marijuana-note emanated from him. Claire got the impression that the young parents were passing their days quite happily in this cocoon of animal warmth and smells: as if they were playing house, everything changed and simplified, revolving around the new life. A tiny baby in a blue Babygro was asleep against his father's naked, muscled brown chest, curled with his head down like a comma.

— Sleeps like a dream all day, keeps me up at night. Give him over, Ben. Make us a cup of tea. This is my Auntie Claire.

— Hello, Auntie Claire.

— Or we could open a bottle? Claire suggested.

— Give the baby to her, she needs a cuddle. I'm not supposed to drink anything fizzy, am I, in case it gives him wind. I'm not going on with this breastfeeding lark for long, whatever Mum thinks. If I put him onto formula, then Ben can get up with him in the night.

Ben lifted the baby in one hand with easy confidence, supporting his lolling head as he handed him over, still sleeping, flushed with heat from his father's chest. No wonder Ben had his T-shirt off, they had the central heating turned up very high, goodness knows what that was costing Susan. Claire dropped her bags and took the damp live package of baby anxiously where she stood, putting all her effort into holding it safely – taking in the loose limbs like a doll's, the tiny frowning face and liver-dark pursed lips, the curve of his eyeballs under the fine skin of his closed lids. His eyebrows were faint exquisite brushstrokes. He stirred and mewed against her and Claire thought he was going to cry; the helplessness of babies disturbed her. — He's beautiful, she exclaimed, not quite sincerely, half repelled by the smothering sour smell.

— Like I said, you can have him, Amy said. She came in with wine glasses from the little kitchen space at the back, more like a scullery. Although some of the walls in the house had been painted and there was a new IKEA

135

sofa, Claire could see that the kitchen units were the same cheap wood veneer ones their mother had bought in the 1980s, when Claire and Susan were at school. A door was missing from one of the cupboards, exposing the piles of bowls and plates.

— My auntie's come all this way just to have a look at His Lordship. Don't you think she'll be disappointed?

— He's pretty boring, Ben said. — He doesn't do much. I was expecting more.

Claire thought he looked at her with curiosity: perhaps she wasn't as he'd imagined Susan's sister, if he'd imagined her at all. Susan was only three years older, but she'd stopped bothering with her appearance – Claire had seen the photographs. She cut her hair herself and hennaed it out of a packet, just like they did when they were teenagers; her face was sagging into lines of worry and her cheekbones were sharp knobs jutting out under the skin. Amy began hunting for pictures on her phone, of the baby in his football outfit. When Claire said that she could remember holding Amy when she was no bigger than Calum, that it seemed like yesterday, Amy was hardly interested – for her, clearly, the history of babies had begun all over again with this one, nothing that had happened before could compare with it.

— She's grown a bit since then, Ben said.

She flicked at him with a tea towel, more interested in her photographs – there seemed to be hundreds of them, though the baby was only a few weeks old. Ben knew how to open champagne, he said he was working part-time in a bar; he was a swaggering performer, full

136

of flourishes. It was easy to see why Amy was attracted to him, and why Susan had been set against him at first: he was one of those boys who traded on their suggestive, languorous flirting. Claire knew that he'd been in trouble – over some minor drug dealing, and then when he'd had an apprenticeship with a Ford dealer until they'd caught him selling spare parts on eBay. Susan had blamed him for Amy's lack of ambition – but now he was living here with them, forgiven, part of the family. When the champagne was poured they all chinked glasses and Claire sipped cautiously, then put her glass down – it was the first alcohol she'd touched since Saturday night, and anyway she was intensely concentrated on the heated bundle in her arms, afraid of somehow dropping or hurting him.

The baby began writhing, his tiny face scrunched up in petulance. When he gave a bleating, penetrating cry, it was a relief to hand him back to Amy, who casually pulled up her top and tugged up her bra, offering him her swollen breast – this seemed too huge at first for him to find his way to the nipple, though he snuffled and gobbled for it desperately. Ben bent over the mother and child and made encouraging smacking noises with his lips. It was impossible to think of that breast now as having any part in sex or desire. Claire topped up their glasses and chatted; she was working hard to charm these young people. It was almost like a continuation of the last few days, putting herself across forcefully while giving an impression that she was making no effort at all – first in the board factory in Chingford, then with the service team in Northampton.

The company she worked for made instruments for testing various materials – paper, plastic film and textiles – measuring thickness and tensile strength. Her role was in cultivating their long-term relationships with the manufacturers who used these instruments; she had to coax people into doing what she knew would work best for them. Now here she was handling her own family using some of the same tactics. At just the right moment she handed out the presents she had brought: offhandedly, as if they'd only been a passing thought. In this world of her home, where everyone was so quick to take offence or feel condescended to, she mustn't seem to be throwing her money around.

Amy felt the quality of the wool shawl appreciatively, still holding the baby to her breast. She said it would be perfect for the christening. — Mum's getting us the christening gown.

— He's going to be christened?

— You know what Mum's like.

— Do I?

— Otherwise she'd be worrying about his eternal soul or something.

Claire was careful not to sound too surprised. — Susan used to be dead set against anything to do with the church.

— Maybe she used to be.

Amy grew evasive then, as if she didn't want to talk about her mother – although when she Skyped Claire in America it was usually to complain over some conflict with Susan. But it was different talking here, in this house. And she'd never mentioned before that Susan had found religion. — She changed, didn't she, after Nanny died.

— That makes sense, Claire said. — Of course.

— She has to have something to hold on to.

— She works too hard, Ben said. — They take advantage of her at that place. They take the piss, seriously.

Susan worked as a carer, visiting elderly and disabled people in their homes, helping them with washing and dressing. Something made Claire uneasy in how Amy and Ben spoke about her sister, turning her into some kind of saint: worn down, put upon, patient and endlessly giving. She recognised a tone of voice in which people had once talked about their own mother, hers and Susan's. They had reacted against that tone when they were teenagers, hating something sanctimonious in it – and dreading that they would have to become this kind of woman in their turn. Now Ben and Amy explained indignantly how, because of the government's austerity cuts, funding for social care had been cut to the bone – the carers were only allowed fifteen minutes for each visit, and weren't even paid for the time it took to drive from one appointment to the next. But Ben was strong and young and capable; if he had contributed more to the household income, Claire thought, then Susan could have cut back on her hours. Everyone loaded all this long-suffering virtue onto their mother figure, to save themselves from trying any harder.

Ryan arrived back from the sixth-form college, where he was studying for his A levels; Claire saw how he exchanged quick glances with Amy as soon as he saw her, and took his cue from his sister – they acted as if there had never been any dreadful falling-out, and it was the most natural thing in the world that their aunt was sitting here at home with them. Ryan was a sweet-natured, odd-looking boy – his face still the big, open child's face Claire remembered, attached now to a man-sized body. He and Ben were pleased with the T-shirts she had brought – she had guessed that Ryan needed extra-large. Amy liked her perfume. When Ben was going to go out in the garden to smoke, he pretended to wrap himself up in the baby's new shawl for warmth, and she was outraged. — I don't want him stinking of fucking weed at his christening.

— Swear box, swear box, said Ryan reproachfully.

Amy explained that the swear box was going towards Calum's education; Ben said he'd be able to afford fucking Eton at this rate. Ryan lifted the baby expertly onto his shoulder, patting its back to bring up wind, putting on a comical posh voice to talk to it. — I say, Ponsonby-Warner, old chap, how was dinner?

When the baby delivered a satisfying burp they laughed with delight.

Claire thought warmly then how good they were – her family – at this baby business. So many of her middle-class friends, in England and America, made such a meal of it: they bought all the baby books and knew all the good advice but the arrival of babies was somehow ruinous in their lives: they grew nagging and crabbed, resentful of the loss of all their fun. Their young children gained the wrong kind of dominion over them, needing to be endlessly coaxed and negotiated with, ferried backwards and forwards to their ballet classes and violin lessons. But Amy had been so inspired and so quick when she was a tiny girl, entertaining the family with her naughty Spice Girls imitations, dressed up in a tacky pink fairy outfit at the Muni – the Municipal Club, where they used to go because Claire and Susan's father was big in the rail union.

— Can I have another cuddle? Claire said. — I don't get enough of this.

Tenderly Ryan handed him over, putting him up on her shoulder where he slumped, content. — Mind he doesn't flob all down you, Ben said; he tucked a muslin cloth solicitously under the baby's head and into the neck of her dress at the back and she felt his fingers faintly – inoffensively – flirty and caressing. Probably the champagne had gone to her head, just the least little bit. While they were all still laughing, they didn't hear Susan come in through the front door. Then she was calling out to her grandson in the midst of all their laughter, while she was hanging up her coat in the hall – they couldn't see her yet, she couldn't see them. For an uncanny moment Claire seemed to hear her mother's old sing-song voice, performing her old role. — Who's my bestest bestest boy in the whole wide world then?

— That was me, once, Ryan drily said.

— Who's Nanny's little darling? Has he been a very good boy today, has he?

When Susan came into the room she was already reaching out her arms to scoop up the baby. Then she saw that Claire was there, that she was holding him: Susan stopped still, her arms dropped by her sides, and the smiles on her face all shut down.

What had happened was this. When Susan's husband left her she'd moved back with her four children into this house, which their parents owned – their father had worked all his life on the railway, and had saved enough out of his wages to put down a deposit and then pay off a mortgage over the years. They had always been proud to own a house, in a street where most of the properties were rented. Then Susan had nursed both their parents through their last illnesses – Claire was still living in London then, and helped out when she could, but of course Susan took the brunt of it. After their mother died, Susan took it for granted that she could go on living in the family home, although in their parents' wills it had been left to both daughters equally. She had never paid any rent, in all those years. Claire had wanted the money to put down on a flat in London – the one she still owned, and had sublet while she was living in the US – and she suggested that Susan could raise a mortgage on the house, to buy her out of her half. Actually she hadn't even asked for half, she'd asked for a lot less. And Susan had done this, but had stopped speaking to her.

When Susan saw Claire, she turned round without even looking at the baby or anyone, and went upstairs to shut herself in her bedroom, slamming the door.

— I'd better go, Claire said.

— Don't be daft. Amy was righteous. — You stay. It's her problem. I don't know why she's being such a cow.

— It was all my fault.

— It was years ago, Ryan said. — She ought to get over it.

— I've tried again and again to say I was sorry. You know I wanted to pay her the money back, and she wouldn't take it?

Embarrassed, they didn't want to hear about the money. — You're not going anywhere, Amy said. — We're going to talk her round. This is an opportunity.

— I thought if she just came in and found me here, it might be all right.

Even as Claire explained in her reasonable calm voice, ripe with regret, she was aware of trying to win them over. This version of what had happened wasn't in the least how Susan saw it. Susan thought there was something monstrous in Claire's selfishness: to turn her back on her family, go south in pursuit of her career and leave her sister to the whole work of nursing their mam and daddy – and then, when they were gone, to demand her share of the property! But Claire was convinced that it had been reasonable, in fact, for her to ask for her share. She had needed a home, too. She had worked very hard to get on in the life she'd chosen, and that inheritance, small as it was, had been her only opportunity to start on the property ladder in London. Perhaps there had been something manic, though, in how she'd insisted on her rights at that time when they were both of them raw from the loss of their mother.

143

She also knew that however she succeeded in charming Susan's children, and however indignant they grew over Susan's stubbornness, deep down their loyalty to her was tribal – Claire could never wheedle her way round it. They thought they knew Susan. But Claire knew her better: this bitter old fight, not at all in keeping with the saintly mother they believed in, had begun long before there was any quarrel over inheritance. Susan hadn't planned on becoming saintly. In another lifetime, it might have been her who left and Claire who stayed. When Susan was seventeen or eighteen, you'd have thought she'd be the one, with her gelled-up hennaed hair and wild politics – she was the one who'd scared their parents and stayed out all night, or come home sodden with drink. There wasn't any particular moment at which that changed, it wasn't when she gave up her A levels or met her husband or had her first babies. Or it was because of all of those things. She had somehow drifted into becoming a good girl.

They took it in turns to try and coax Susan out. Her room now was the small back bedroom which had once been Claire's: the double room at the front was given over to Amy and Ben and the baby. Unfortunately this back room had a bolt on the inside – Claire had fixed it herself, when she was going through a private phase – so they had to remonstrate with Susan through the closed door. Ryan took her up a glass from the second bottle of champagne, Amy stood outside with Calum, putting on a baby voice, begging her to come out, telling her she

144

was being a daft bugger. She wouldn't speak, except to ask them whether Claire was gone. — I'll come down when she's gone out of this house, she said, as melodramatic as if she were in a book. It was as though she seized this licence to be excessive and unreasonable, in return for all the years of putting herself last.

The bathroom was built on at the back of the house, on the ground floor, beyond the kitchen; surely she'd have to come down sooner or later, Ryan said – she must be busting up there. When Amy began cooking supper, Claire offered to take over, and made spaghetti and mince with what was in the fridge. She could have found her way around that kitchen in the dark – though it wasn't dark, their daddy had put in a glaring neon light. Her hands remembered like old friends, or old enemies, how the knife-and-fork drawer stuck, and how to adjust the knobs on the temperamental electric cooker, whose markings had worn away long ago. She served up for everyone, putting out some dinner for Susan too. The dining table had been moved into the front room, so the young ones had their plates on their laps in front of the telly.

Shutting the door deliberately behind her, Claire took Susan's plate upstairs and stood adjusting to the quiet on the landing, in the near-dark; she thought she could feel her sister breathing, out of sight. In the tension the two of them must each be listening out for the other, half hating and half exulting – like in the old days when they'd acted up together, playing out some game, swelling with the laughter that must not erupt. Trying the stainless-steel handle, holding onto the plate of spaghetti with its fork, she put her whole weight against the door, which wouldn't give. Then she spoke into the crack of the frame, the gloss paint cool against her cheek, feeling the power of what was withheld on the other side. Its resistance to her was fundamental, primal. — Sue? If you'll just let me in for one moment, I promise I'll go. I don't want anything. I only want to see you. I brought you something to eat.

The silence and stillness persisted, obdurate as something material between them. She rattled at the handle, then put her free hand flat against the door and felt as if she was receiving some signal through her palm from inside the room: alongside the resentment there was recognition, she was sure of it. — Let me in, I know you're listening to me, she said.

All evening she kept up her entertainment of Susan's family. Ben went round to the shop with a twenty-pound note she gave him for more drink, Amy supplied all the grisly details of the birth, they discussed Amy and Ryan's older sisters – a nurse and a teaching assistant, both living in Manchester. They talked about Ryan's girlfriend and Ben's plans – and films they'd seen, and TV soaps. They were all full of plans. Claire was good at taking an interest in other people's lives. She said a little bit about America when they asked her, not making too much of the things she preferred about living over there. All the time she was distracting them from worrying about their mother upstairs. When she said she ought to go, and asked about hotels in town, Amy insisted she wasn't staying anywhere except right here.

Their conversation was relaxed – maybe the television helped, because it was always on. They had playback, so they could be tuned in all the time to their favourite smart comedies, American and British; perhaps partly because of these programmes, their own humour seemed quick and sophisticated to Claire – she was impressed. If the baby fussed he was passed around between them and they all took their turn at soothing him, walking up and down with him and jigging him; Ben changed his nappy and everyone watched around the changing mat as if Calum were a little prince at court. The sight of his weak flailing baby limbs and the reddened swollen navel tugged painfully at Claire – he startled fearfully once, jerking his whole body with a grimace and lost cry as if he were falling through empty space. From time to time they took up mugs of tea for Susan which she didn't drink, or tried to talk to her through the closed door. When they marvelled at how Susan was managing without visiting the bathroom, Amy remembered she kept Nanny's old pot under the bed, in case she was caught short in the night: the boys protested that was more information than they needed.

Amy found sheets for Claire to put on the pull-out sofa in the front room – Ryan offered her his bedroom but she said she'd rather be downstairs. The small front room was crowded with odds and ends of furniture, broken hi-fi, boxes of china wrapped in newspaper; there were even a couple of bikes propped against one wall. The footsteps of passers-by sounded intimately close outside the window. The same old sunburst clock – against the Anaglypta wallpaper, above the gas fire with its teak surround – was stopped perpetually at ten past four. Claire made up the sofa bed and put out her clothes for the morning on a hanger. Then when the others had all finished in the bathroom, she felt herself in possession of the house at last, prowling round the ground floor in her stockinged feet, washing the dishes in the kitchen, tidying up quietly. The noise of television or the Internet seeped from the rooms upstairs, the baby bleated once or twice and then was stilled.

When she went out to listen in the hall, Claire noticed for the first time a red bag on the floor, made of thick imitation leather with strong handles, crammed untidily full; this had to be Susan's work bag, she must have put it down when she came in. Soundlessly she picked it up and took it into the front room, shutting the door behind her. Then she lifted things out of the bag one after another onto her bed, scrupulous to preserve their exact order – folders and a phone and an umbrella and a street map; car keys and a purse and woollen gloves and a hairbrush full of dead hair; a Tupperware box with half a sandwich and a KitKat uneaten inside it. She laid the silk scarf that she'd bought for her sister, still wrapped in its tissue paper, in the very bottom of the bag, hidden under a few scuffed old leaflets and a plastic rain hat. Very carefully then, so no one could tell that anything had been disturbed, she replaced everything else on top of it, and returned the bag to its place under the coats. It might be months even, she thought, before Susan found her present. But when she did, she'd know who put it there.

She picked up a newspaper from the magazine rack; it was days old, folded open to where a cryptic crossword was half finished in Susan's handwriting. Claire wanted to complete it; she hunted for a biro and made herself more tea and a hot-water bottle and got into her bed, frowning over the clues one after another. Their mother had been good at crosswords, squinting at them through the smoke from her Embassy Regal; Susan had learned from her how to write out her anagrams like this in circles, breaking up the pattern of the original words and allowing new ones to emerge. Filling in with satisfaction the letters that fitted around Susan's letters, Claire felt herself closely in contact with her sister and expected to hear her coming down at any moment. No matter how quietly she moved, the creaking stairs would give her away. As soon as she heard Susan, Claire thought, she would get out of bed just as she was in her nightdress and follow her into the back room and speak to her, and they would surely be able to find their way through all this rubble of the past piled up between them. But she couldn't finish the crossword, and fell asleep over it eventually.

In the morning she woke very early. When she got up from her sofa bed to use the bathroom before the others needed it, she saw that the red bag and Susan's coat were gone from the hall; she must have left for work already, although it was still dark, not six o'clock. Perhaps Claire

149

had been aware in her sleep of the front door quietly opening and closing, Susan's car starting up outside. It would be for the best if she left too, she calculated, before the sleepy household creaked into action. She was keen now to return to her own world. The baby began to squeak upstairs and she heard Amy grumbling, picking him up out of his crib. Quickly Claire washed at the sink in the bathroom, then dressed and tidied the sofa bed away, folding up the sheets and the duvet, bundling yesterday's clothes into her shoulder bag. The idea of another day spent attending to the baby in that stuffy room made her feel panic. She wrote a note for Amy in the kitchen.

When she closed the front door behind her and stepped out into the grey light in the empty street, filling her lungs with foggy air, she felt the same exulting relief she always had, since she first left when she was seventeen. A bus ran from a stop just round the corner, which would take her to the station. She'd reserved a room in the same hotel near Liverpool Street; that night she was going out for a meal with London friends. Her flight the next day didn't leave until the early afternoon. In Philadelphia she'd have to face the work colleague she'd slept with before she came away – but she could cope with that, and get over it. He was married with children, so he was unlikely to have told anyone. She was ashamed to remember how she'd begun that evening by flirting with this man and teasing him, believing herself in charge of what could happen; now certain bloody, humiliating truths seemed indelible between them. But you could shed your skin over and over, Claire thought, and believe each time that you'd come to the end of shame, and it wasn't true. You could always be born again, with a new skin. She hadn't come to the end of her chances, not yet.

When she arrived at the hotel in London they didn't have her room ready, so she left her suitcase at reception and sat in the lounge with a coffee and a mineral water, putting some of the notes she'd made in Chingford into the form of a report which would be useful for her boss, tapping away on her laptop, checking emails. A suspicion darted suddenly through her preoccupation. She unzipped the shoulder bag on the seat beside her, riffling among the dirty clothes and nightdress and wash things. When she found what she was hunting for – there at the bottom of the bag was the silk scarf, untouched in its tissue paper – she actually laughed out loud. Incredible! How had Susan guessed that the scarf was hidden in her own bag? Of course if anyone could outwit her it was her sister. But how ever had she managed to creep into the front room while Claire slept, and hide it again among her things without waking her?

For a moment Claire only wanted to get rid of the little package. She could leave it behind her here in the lounge when she went upstairs, or drop it into the waste bin in her room, a surprise for the cleaner. Then she changed her mind. After all, she could keep the scarf for herself. Why not? Tearing off the tissue paper, she lifted it out of its folds. The heavy, slippery silk

151

flooded into her lap, lithe and vivid as an animal; it was nicer even than she'd remembered, the tan and green colours making her think of woodland and fresh leaves. When she put it around her neck its touch was subtle, cool. She felt a moment's stabbing sorrow for everything she'd lost and left behind. But she knew from past experience how to push that sorrow down and bury it.

Under the Sign of
the Moon

The train paused at a red light on its way into the station, waiting for a platform to clear. The passengers had put on their coats and put away their laptops and lifted their bags down from the luggage rack; some were already standing, queuing between the seats. Liverpool was the last station, the end of the two-and-a-half-hour journey from London; they were ready to move on but could not move anywhere yet. Quiet and stillness settled unexpectedly on the carriage. Because the forward motion of their lives was suspended while they waited, the passengers were suddenly more intimately present to one another – although no one spoke or made eye contact. Greta felt the change in atmosphere and looked up from her book and out of the window, keeping her finger on her page. They were waiting in shadow, in a cutting between high walls of red sandstone.

In the rock she could see, like art patterns following the natural lines of the strata, the chisel marks of the navvies who'd once cut and blasted down into it. The rock face was streaked with moss, and here and there buddleia and fern had rooted, scrawny because they lived out their lives in this subterranean railway kingdom; far above, ash saplings stood out against a pale sky. The strata in the rock were woven into sections of brick wall and the old bricks – small and vivid, rust-coloured, crusted with salts – seemed to flow as if they, too, had been put down in sedimentary layers. Elegantly arched recesses were built into the base of the wall. The old engineering was as magnificent in its scale and ambition as a Roman ruin, Greta thought, its ancientness inscrutable and daunting and moving.

The man sitting across the table from her noticed that she was looking out. He told her that this was the oldest stretch of railway in the world, and that they used to have to haul the trains into Lime Street from here, because it was too steep for the early locomotives. — There are stables built into the rock for all the horses, he said. — We're inside a hill they call Mount Olive.

Greta didn't know whether she believed him: whether he was the sort of man who knew about things or the sort who made them up. She made an interested noise, then looked back down at her book without speaking. Since her illness began, at least in the intervals when she felt well enough to read, she had immersed herself in books almost fanatically, trying not to leave open any chink in her consciousness through which she could be waylaid by awareness of her body or by fear or disgust. She read only fiction, not history or politics, and nothing experimental or difficult that would require her to pause for reflection or argument. She had read a lot of novels recently that she would have disdained in the past.

As soon as she had settled into her seat at Euston, the man across the table had shown signs of wanting to talk. He had asked her how far she was going, and then whether she was travelling for business or on a holiday. Greta had answered, friendly enough, that she was going to see her daughter, Kate, who had moved to Liverpool recently. It hadn't occurred to her at first that he might want their conversation to continue past these preliminaries. The gap between them had seemed too immense; she was almost sixty, and he was surely nearer to her daughter's age. His rather distinctive hair was short and thick: dark blond, wavy and wiry, with burnished gold threads in it. When he found out that Kate lived in Aigburth, he told her that he was born there, and seemed disproportionately astonished and delighted by the coincidence. Greta couldn't hear any traces of a Liverpool accent, but he might have shed it or never had it.

There was something in his eagerness to please that warned her off. His good looks reminded her of certain damaged film stars and pop stars from her childhood in the early sixties: cheekbones and jaw chiselled too rigidly, mouth loose-lipped and needy, handsome head oversized in relation to the slack, slight body. He was neatly dressed: none of Kate's male friends would ever have chosen to wear a belted short white mac, an open-necked yellow shirt and a maroon V-necked jumper. If Greta hadn't heard the man speak she might have thought he was a foreigner, a Central European, dressing according to a different code. He took the mac off at some point and folded it, laying it carefully on the seat beside him, on top of a leather box-briefcase with a combination lock. You didn't see those briefcases so often now, she realised, because everybody carried a laptop. The briefcase was old-fashioned, like his clothes.

He kept telling her how much she was going to like Liverpool. It had a reputation, he said, but actually it had changed completely since the bad old days. Liverpudlians were the most warm-hearted people you'd ever meet; they'd give you their last crust if you needed it. Greta thought she could hear the accent then, slipping into his speech – almost as if he were putting it on for her benefit. The only thing she didn't like about Liverpool, she thought, was the way people who came from there harped on about how warm-hearted they were. She didn't bother to tell him that she had visited Kate once already, a year ago, just after her diagnosis. And she had lived in Liverpool for a while, too, in the seventies, with Kate's father – who was not the man she was married to now. So she knew something about how much the city had changed.

Determinedly, she opened up her book.

— I can see you're a great reader, he said.

— Yes.

— I wish I had more time for it. I used to love stories when I was a kid. Mum said the world could end while I was reading and I wouldn't even notice.

Smiling non-committally, she pretended to be wrapped up at once in her novel – though for a few moments the words she stared at swam in her mind, not conveying any meaning. She was too aware of her companion's presence across the table, and of having so firmly cut off his desire to talk. He seemed at a loss as to what to do without her. He didn't even have a newspaper with him. But Greta had to save herself, and didn't care if he thought she was rude or cold.

He didn't show any sign of being offended. He spoke to her again from time to time – usually when, having forgotten about him, she looked up inadvertently from her reading. — How's it going? he asked jocularly once, nodding at her book as if it were a marathon test she'd set herself. The train stopped at Stafford, and he seemed to know all about that, too – he told her about a castle, and a battle in the Civil War. Was she imagining things, or did she detect faint traces then of a Midlands accent? He might be one of those chameleons, changing his coloration to match wherever he was. When he went to get coffee from the buffet he offered to bring one for her, too; she longed for coffee but refused, because she knew she'd feel obliged to pay for it with conversation.

She would have been quite sure, once, that this man was trying to chat her up – there was a certain persistent, burrowing sweetness in his attentions. However, that was out of the question now. When Greta put on her reading glasses to look in the mirror these days, she saw that her skin was papery and sagged on her neck and under her jaw, her face was criss-crossed by tiny creases. This wasn't all the effect of her illness; much of it was just ordinary ageing. She had spent yesterday afternoon at the hairdresser's, having her hair cut and highlighted so that she could present a cheerful, sanely coping front to Kate, but still her brown hair was full of grey. Also, Greta couldn't help believing that her problems, which were gynaecological, showed on the surface somehow, barring her definitively from the world of sexual attraction. That part of her life was over. She didn't want to read online about women who'd had what she had and gone on to enjoy exciting sex lives for years afterwards. She dreaded the smiling pretence even more than the bleak truth.

When Greta wheeled her suitcase off the platform and onto the main Liverpool concourse, she expected to catch sight of Kate at once. The rush of emotion in this expectation took her by surprise: most of her feelings, over these past months, had been muted, as if she were persisting through grim effort. She anticipated with her whole body the instant when she would see Kate and they would be enfolded together; looking keenly around, she seemed to see her daughter already stepping forward – handsome, tall, spirited – out of the crowd. They weren't the kind of mother and daughter who were always cuddling and touching, but surely they would embrace now, after everything that had happened.

Then she heard her phone ping and had to rummage for it in her handbag and put her glasses on to read the text. Kate would be about twenty minutes late – no hint of regret or apology. And Greta knew Kate: twenty minutes meant half an hour, at least. Her disappointment as she read was infantile. What did it matter if Kate was a bit late? But the idea of her daughter's waiting for her had seemed for a moment like a rich gift of the good luck she had got used to doing without. She had been trying so sedulously not to want anything too much. Quickly she wiped her eyes with a tissue from her sleeve. Nothing had gone wrong; everything was still on track. She could use the time to get herself the coffee she had wanted earlier. Wheeling her suitcase over to one of the café franchises in the station, she didn't see until the last minute that her companion from the train was there ahead of her, sitting at a table out on the concourse, beside the dark little den where the coffee was made.

He hadn't seen her, either: he was bending his head over his coffee, blowing on it to cool it. At least she couldn't accuse him of stalking her; it looked now, if anything, as if she were in pursuit of him. Away from the train, with his mac on and a paisley silk scarf tied around his neck, he didn't seem quite so unfortunate; there was even something touchingly contained and self-sufficient in the way he sat absorbed in the steam from his cup, not texting or talking on his phone, no phone in evidence at all. His skin was rough and pitted, but the slanting lines and planes of his cheekbones were striking in profile, beautiful like those of a peasant in an old

Central European photograph, though Greta thought he didn't know it. When he did notice her – a wheel on her suitcase got caught on the leg of one of the wrought-iron cafe chairs, scraping it along the floor – he put down his cup with what appeared to be genuine pleasure at seeing her again. Concerned, he asked if everything was all right. Probably her nose was flushed red – that was usually what happened when she cried. She explained brightly that her daughter had been delayed, and she'd decided to have a coffee while she waited.

On an impulse, she paused beside his table. — Do you mind if I sit here?

He leaped to pull out a chair for her. — Be my guest.

This time, Greta allowed him to buy her a coffee, a cappuccino; he went to queue for it at the counter inside. Actually, she was grateful; she needed to sit down. She wasn't in pain, exactly: there was only the deep ache where her womb once was, and a familiar draining sensation as if her blood were waves, dragging at the gravel on a shore. There was no need to hold herself so carefully apart from this stranger, she thought, just because he was needy and lonely. She was needy, too. They might as well keep each other company.

He was keen to talk about himself, when Greta encouraged him. He had come to Liverpool to visit relatives who lived in Blundellsands, but they wouldn't be home from work yet so he was in no hurry; he would have a little look around before he caught the bus. He had only a small suitcase with him, she saw, along with the briefcase. These relatives weren't his own age; they were his mother's cousins. Greta began to guess that he was one of those people who spent their youth involved with an older generation, until they themselves became elderly by association – and didn't mind it in the least or try to escape. This would explain his clothes, and something quaint and dated in his manner. She could imagine him as the cherished boy in a strong, extended family, which for no particular reason hadn't produced many children. Such a good, obedient boy, and so nice-looking: they would be bemused by the fact that he didn't have more friends his own age, or a girlfriend. Greta enquired about girlfriends and he reddened, said he was afraid not, not at present. He might be gay: she had already wondered about that.

He worked for his uncle, who managed a small wholesaler's in Brentford, supplying foil containers and other utensils to the food trade. The Liverpool relatives had invited him to stay because he needed a change of scene: he was still getting over the shock of his mother's death, six months ago. He and his mother had been very close, he said; he had lived at home to keep her company after his father died. It was easy to assume that families like this didn't exist any more: submissive, frugal, unpolitical, tribal. Greta knew for certain, as though she'd seen it, that last night he had laid out his clothes for the journey, along with his train ticket, just as his mother would have done for him when she was alive, and that he had checked several times to be sure he hadn't forgotten anything. This was the world of Greta's childhood, which she had rejected so absolutely. She knew that the tragic story of his mother's visits to the GP, her misdiagnosis and her falling down unconscious in the street while she was shopping must have been recounted many times: it was as well worn as the track of footsteps around an old carpet. You could feel the reality collapsing into the familiar safe phrases, becoming part of a routine, becoming myth: — The nurses in the hospital were very kind. They did everything they could. She looked very peaceful when they laid her out.

Then Greta lifted her head and saw Kate in the distance.

— Ah, here's my daughter! she cried, triumphant, interrupting him, half standing up from the table to wave to Kate. She knew it was unseemly of her to abandon him like that mid-sentence: he was telling her something so intimate and so important to him, and she had encouraged him to tell her these things, had skilfully probed for them. Kate was wearing silky loose trousers, a cropped top tight across her breasts, showing her bare midriff, and some kind of military-style coat with yellow frogging, hanging open. She was the very opposite type to Greta's new friend, not in the least meek or old-fashioned. The long rope of her hair, worn in a ponytail high on her head, was red by nature, dyed with streaks of a wilder red. Catching sight of Greta, she strode across the concourse towards her, impatient as if she weren't the one who was late. — I don't have the car, she announced, only glancing disparagingly at her mother's companion. — Boyd needed it today. We have to get a taxi.

Kate always had an air of submitting to her mother's kisses, rather than returning them: her quickly proffered cheek tasted of moisturiser, the skin so clear. There was hardly time for Greta to say goodbye to the young man, and they parted as if it were the merest accident that they'd been sitting at the same table. She hadn't properly looked at him again, once she'd seen Kate. And yet, while she was smiling proudly, watching Kate make her way towards them, he had said something fairly astonishing – so quickly, and with such an air of its being an acceptable and reasonable suggestion, that Greta wasn't sure at first that she'd heard correctly. Then she didn't have time to respond before Kate was there, taking charge. He'd said that he would be at the Palm House in Sefton Park on Thursday afternoon at two o'clock. If she wanted, she could meet him there.

When Greta lived in Liverpool, in the seventies, with her first husband, before Kate was born – in fact the very summer Kate was conceived – she wasn't called Greta. Her name then was Margaret: Maggie. And Ian, Kate's father, wasn't strictly Greta's husband, either, not by law. It was while they were staying with friends in that squat in Liverpool that they had devised their own marriage ceremony. *Under the sign of the moon and the eye of the goddess*, it began. *With my body I thee worship.* It was difficult to know, with Ian, just how much irony there was in this. He could be pretty mocking about phoney mysticism. He knew about the real pagans, he said: he had read classics at York University, which was where he and Greta had met, though Ian had dropped out halfway through their second year. And he had a way of inciting other people to behave extravagantly, then looking on with gleeful amusement, as if he couldn't believe how biddable they were.

Ian and Greta made little cuts on their thumbs in front of their friends in the squat, and mingled bloods, and ate their food from the same dish. He was smaller than she was, very skinny and lithe and excitable, always jumping about like a kid, with a silky beard and very pale skin and the same silky auburn hair as Kate's. Sometimes he was exquisitely kind to Greta – especially in sex, but not only then. He loved it when she absorbed herself in his crazes, for planting things or baking bread or Hungarian folk music; they had talked seriously about moving to Wales together, to try subsistence farming. She had learned never to relax her guard, though. He could snatch his favour away from one moment to the next, retreating into a dark mood, leaving her bereft.

Ian dropped acid for the first time on their wedding day, along with a gang of their friends. Greta was too afraid to try it, but said she would stay with the others to watch out for them. They went wandering around the streets at night, exclaiming over all the ordinary sights: telephone boxes and cars and garden shrubs. All natural things were beautiful; everything man-made seemed monstrous. Ian announced that he could see into the atomic structure of the paving stones under their feet, which was like a fluorescent grid of energy: he could have sunk through it if he'd wanted, but he consented to the laws of physics, allowing it to hold him up. They climbed over a fence into a park – it might have been Sefton Park – and headed for the open grassy slopes, where they lay on their backs looking up at the sky. Some of the boys built a fire out of fallen branches and stood talking to it. — Brother fire, we won't hurt you, they said. They found it funny and profound when someone asked whether the fire was heating them or they were heating the fire.

Then Ian wanted Greta to consummate the marriage with him there on the grass, in honour of the moon goddess: except that there wasn't a moon, the night was cloudy and the grass was wet. Obviously they had had sex many times before – but he insisted that this time was sacred. Greta said that she couldn't, because of the others being there.

— Don't be afraid, he said, coaxing her, lying half on top of her, rubbing her breast with his palm, covering her neck with little nibbling kisses. — Trust me: Margaret, Maggie, Marguerite. It will be different, because we're man and wife. It will be amazing. Don't be uptight, don't be bourgeois.

He often teased her for being bourgeois. His own family was far nastier than Greta's – his father was a bully who worked for the BBC, and his mother was an actress and an alcoholic. But perhaps it was worse to be safe and dull. Their lovemaking would be beautiful for everyone to see, he told her. — Knock knock, open up.

— How come your title doesn't change, Greta said, — and mine does? You're still man, but I'm wife? Why don't you call yourself husband?

165

Her feminism in those days consisted mostly of these niggling technicalities. Usually Ian tolerated them, as if they were of no importance. Now he stopped kissing her but stayed on top of her, his hand still on her breast; his breath on her cheek smelled sour. He was looking through the dark into her face – not at it but into it. Up to that point she had wondered whether the tab of acid was really having any effect on him, because he had sounded too much like himself, putting on what he imagined tripping ought to be like.

– I can see into your thoughts, he said. – I can see them pulsing. I can see the little petty, sulky worms of your thoughts, eating you up because you're dead. Poor little Maggie, everyone. So pretty, isn't she? But I found out she's dead.

For a moment, Greta seemed to see what Ian saw, as if she were looking down at herself. The whole sum of her being had a kind of corpse-luminescence in the darkness: stiff and mechanical, inhibited. Because of her background, or perhaps just because of her intrinsic nature, there were certain levels of experience she would never be able to attain; she would never break out of the bounds of her reasonable self. Then she pushed him away and sat up and was upset and angry, and he ignored her, cutting her out of conversations as if she weren't there.

The others all seemed by now to have passed into a world she couldn't enter. Eventually she left them to it and made her way back to the squat; she spent her wedding night alone, sobbing and desolate, worrying that something terrible would happen because she'd abandoned them. Nothing terrible did happen – although the police turned up in the park, because of the fire, and chased them out. And she did find out, weeks later, that after she left Ian had made love on the grass anyway, with a girl called Carol, whom they hardly knew: a friend of a friend, passing through the squat. Greta had wondered why Carol left so precipitously the next day. When she confronted Ian, he asked if she thought she owned his body, just because she was married to him. — We're not going to do any of that crap, he said. — And by the way, that trippy sex was amazing – like fucking the universe, for eternity. You should try it sometime. Honestly.

Greta sometimes told stories about Ian to her second husband – the real one, Graham, who came later. Reliably, Graham would be outraged by Ian's arrogance and swaggering selfishness. Whenever the two men crossed paths – Ian would take a fancy, every so often, to being involved in his daughter's upbringing – Ian could be counted on to turn up hours late, to feed Kate the sweets that made her hyper, and to keep her up long past her bedtime, so that she had a sick headache the next day. He condescended with amusement to Greta and Graham's domestic routines. Greta, by this time, was an English teacher at a comprehensive school, and Graham worked with disaffected teenagers. Ian never settled down to anything so steady; for a while he had a business buying old pine furniture and stripping it. It didn't help that when Kate was little she adored her father, who forgot about her for months at a time: it was Graham who pushed her on the swings in the playground, packed her little bag for nursery school, got up with her at night when she had bad dreams.

There was something not quite honest, Greta knew, in the way she prodded Graham to say those dismissive and loathing things about Ian. Partly, it smoothed out certain tricky passages in their relationship, made Graham her defender. Otherwise, he might have wondered how much she still yearned, treacherously, for Ian – because there were aspects of the stories about Ian that she withheld. When he told her, for instance, about the 'trippy sex', Greta had actually laughed, because she knew that he had chosen the word 'trippy' deliberately to flaunt at her, with its plastic, blaring garishness, calculated to make her curl up. Fucking the universe for eternity, really? He couldn't mean it, not in those preposterous words. And when she'd laughed, Ian had laughed too, and their quarrel had finished as usual in vengeful, untender love-making, the two of them gripping hard, staring shamelessly, right to the bitter end, or almost to the end. — Look at you, Ian had said with amazement. — Just look at you.

Ian died when Kate was nine, knocked off his bike by a lorry in London. And these days she didn't want to hear anything about him; she called Graham 'Dad', which she had refused to do when she was a child. In the taxi from the station she chattered insistently, and Greta knew that it was because she was afraid of hearing about her mother's illness. Greta would find that they'd made a few changes in the flat, Kate said. They'd bought a new sofa, and because they couldn't afford a new kitchen they'd painted the cupboard doors a different colour. Greta guessed that Kate was vaguely aggrieved about the new kitchen – her sense of her entitlement to material things was somehow not greedy, just part of her natural force. She and Boyd were doing well at the university: the department had won an important research grant, which would fund their fellowships for at least three more years. Boyd and Kate both worked in Ocean Sciences, Boyd on the carbon cycle, Kate on fish stocks.

Greta sat forward to look out of the taxi window, trying to spot landmarks from the seventies. — I remember once it was dusk, she said, — and we were in a car. I don't know whose car – Ian didn't own one. And the road ran round in front of a great circle of Victorian buildings, so tall they blocked out the sky – so many windows. Huge hotels, perhaps, railway hotels. Then we realised these buildings were empty shells, half ruined – you could see right through them in places. Like being in ancient Rome after the fall of the empire.

The whole idea of her mother's past made Kate uneasy. — Who was that creepy guy you were with at the station? she asked suspiciously. — You were chatting merrily away together.

Greta was practised at presenting a face wiped clean of knowledge. — Just someone who was sitting there when I sat down, she said. — There weren't any empty tables.

— Yes, there were.

It wasn't until Greta's suitcase had been unloaded onto the pavement in front of Kate's flat that Kate asked about her health, hastily, as if in passing. The flat was a recent conversion, in a detached house in a wide street planted with hornbeams, where a few houses were still crazily derelict.

— So what do the doctors say? Are they pleased with you?

Greta was paying the driver. She didn't mind that Kate always asked like this, appealing above her head to the doctors, as if her mother couldn't be trusted to understand her own disease; it was only Kate's way of channelling her emotions. Greta said she thought the doctors were pleased: they didn't want to see her for three months. This was the truth, although she pronounced it with an air of blessed reprieve that wasn't exactly what she felt. Her expectations lately were so muffled and diminished, and there was too much that could happen in three months.

Inside the flat, Kate solicitously made Greta comfortable on the new sofa, put the kettle on for tea; she had bought almond cakes from an organic place Boyd approved of. Kate could forgive her mother for being ill, now that she was allowed not to dread the worst – she could even forgive her for not wanting cake. — You have to eat, you know, Kate said. — You're horribly thin. It doesn't suit you.

Greta closed her eyes, giving herself up to the kettle's roaring undertow, the thud and rattle of the fridge door closing, the chiming of a spoon against china mugs, Kate's low humming to herself, the central-heating radiators coming to life, clicking and easing. Her awareness of her daughter's coming and going was like a thick thread of feeling, connecting them materially. In these past months, her mind would quite often submerge like this in her surroundings. This is all there is, she'd think – being alive, just here, right now. It wasn't a reductive or depressing insight; it was almost a form of happiness, the kind of apprehension religious people strove for.

Away from Boyd, Greta could find herself resenting him; you might have thought he was a tyrant, from Kate's anxious attention to his opinions and judgements. He wouldn't touch alcohol; he only liked European jazz; because of climate change, he refused to fly. But Greta and Graham had scrutinised him with deep suspicion and had to conclude that it was Kate who made the tyranny, for her own purposes – she who had never submitted to anyone before. And if it was tyranny, then she was thriving on it, blooming and softened and eager in his presence.

Boyd arrived home, the first evening of Greta's stay, laden with bags full of meat and vegetables from the farmers' market he'd visited in the morning; he cooked a stir-fry, which was just the thing to appeal to Greta's appetite. And as soon as he was actually present, Greta remembered how much she liked him: fair and trim and rosy, light on his feet, with a neat round head and a bald patch like a monk's tonsure. His fleecy clothes in primary colours were no doubt scientifically designed to keep him warm, or cool, or whatever it was he wanted. He was much better than Kate at asking sensibly how Greta was, and then not making a big deal of it but drawing her into more general conversation, doing her the courtesy of presuming that she was still interested. Boyd was definitely the kind of man who knew things. He had strong opinions, but they were always worth listening to. When Kate held forth about the degradation of the oceans she was indignant, as if it were everyone's fault but hers; Boyd was more measured and realistic. Sometimes Greta even thought he colluded with her in amusement – which Kate didn't notice – at Kate's passionate partisanship. And no doubt his responses to Greta, when she didn't know things or muddled her ideas, were tinged with the same, not ungenerous humour.

The life Kate and Boyd led wasn't anything like Greta's life had been, when she was in her thirties. For instance, Greta and Graham would have chosen to live on this street precisely because of its mixture of renovated houses with derelict ones. They'd liked to feel that they were living on the edge of something 'real', not retreating too far inside the safety of privilege; whereas Boyd explained to Greta, unapologetically, that he and Kate saw this flat as a transitional step on their way to buying a house in a nicer area. And yet this younger couple were more likely to effect radical change in the world, for the good, through their work, than she and Graham ever had been. Their certainty and their energy warmed her – even if she couldn't quite suppress her habit of critical observation. Boyd was comical, sorting the recycling with such earnest pedantry. And Greta enjoyed noticing that he had a weakness for sweet things. After he'd eaten his own almond cake, he finished the one that she had hardly touched.

She asked him about the cutting where her train had waited outside the station. Was it true that it was the oldest railway in the world? Someone had told her it was. Boyd thought it might be – the oldest passenger railway, at least. And, yes, they really had once hauled the trains up the last steep stretch into Lime Street Station, because the old locomotives weren't strong enough. But Boyd was sceptical when she mentioned stables. Horses would never have been strong enough to pull an entire train uphill. No, he thought that there had been some kind of pulley system – wagons laden with ballast going down, pulling up the coaches full of people. The evening began to be filled with their interest. Boyd looked things up on the Internet and read them out to Greta, about the building of the railways and the hard lives of the navvies. He was more or less right, it turned out, about the pulley system; Greta wondered whether she'd misunderstood the man on the train, who had mentioned horses, or whether he'd made a mistake. Kate didn't care about the railways, but she was happy because Boyd wasn't bored; he was enjoying himself.

That night Greta dreamed that she was at the Palm House in Sefton Park – although this wasn't a place she remembered ever having visited in her real life. Her idea of it had obviously got mixed up with the memory of

173

those Victorian hotels in their ruined grandeur; the high walls of the Palm House were precarious and toppling, and inside it was wildly overgrown with the exotic plants that must once have been cultivated there. In her dream, she was pushing through thick foliage – brittle, dusty leaves and clinging creepers and intricately fleshy blooms. And she was aware of someone else moving around nearby, rattling the spiky, dark green leaves, grunting with puzzled and exasperated effort: at any moment they might come face to face. Then she must have wandered out somehow without meaning to. From outside, the Palm House looked more like a glasshouse, crazily dilapidated, its iron frame rusty and festooned with some kind of municipal tape, perhaps meant as a safety warning. A solid mass of plant growth pressed against the steamed-up glass inside and pushed out through broken panes. Dark figures seemed to be standing around the perimeter of the building at intervals, facing outwards as if they were on guard. Greta woke up then, and opened her eyes in the pitch dark. She was on the sofa bed in Kate and Boyd's spare room, which was also their study: lying on her back, which always made her snore. Probably that accounted for the grunting and the exasperated efforts.

Kate had managed to free up some time to spend with her mother, but on the Thursday, as it happened, she needed to go in to work. Greta reassured her that she would be happy spending the day by herself. She would go out for coffee to that friendly place nearby where

Kate had taken her. And if the weather was fine she might manage a stroll in the park afterwards.

On Thursday morning, when Boyd and Kate had gone and she was alone in the flat, Greta took a long time getting ready. She knew she had to pace herself for these efforts; when she took a bath, she was careful not to wet her hair, which still looked all right from the hairdresser's, because washing and drying it would use up too much of her strength. Then she put on the nicest outfit she had brought with her: a dark navy cord skirt and red wool shirt and navy cashmere jumper. She even got out Kate's ironing board and pressed the skirt, which was creased from her suitcase. Sitting at the mirror in Kate's bedroom, she made up her face, beginning with moisturiser, then putting on a very light foundation – which she never used to wear but thought she needed now, to make herself presentable. It seemed significant, but not unbearable, to be confronting her own worn-out face with such purposeful attention – pulling it into the old grimaces, creaming and painting and smudging with her fingertip – in the mirror that usually reflected Kate. In Greta's imagination Kate's youthful looks were somehow balanced against hers, redeeming them. Not that Kate wasted much time staring at her reflection. Her beautifying was still lordly and dismissive: fastening the long tail of her hair in a few quick movements, tugging earrings hastily into her piercings, stooping to the mirror to draw thickly with black eyeliner along her lids, finishing with that bold upward stroke. Kate could have gone naked into the street and been lovely.

The place Greta went for coffee was round the corner from the flat, in a row of independent restaurants and small shops selling home-baked bread and local pottery. A converted chapel offered Pilates and art classes, and Sefton Park was beyond that, at the end of the road. Greta bought a copy of the *Guardian* and found herself a corner by a warm radiator in the shabby red-and-yellow-painted cafe-bar. — It's a hippie place, Mum, Kate had said. — Just your kind of thing.

Students were working on laptops; a couple of men probably Greta's age, with flaring drinkers' faces, had emptied a bottle of wine already, at the bar. Young mothers had escaped from home to gossip with their friends, steering their bulky pushchairs in beside the tables. There was plenty of room – no one would mind if Greta took her time over her coffee. It was a relief to be away from Graham for a while, she thought, though the thought wasn't drastic or hostile: she never wavered, these days, in her appreciation of his kindness. When she looked at her watch at a quarter to two, she decided to buy herself a second cup of coffee; then, on impulse, at the bar she asked for a glass of Pinot Grigio instead, though that was risky in the middle of the day. She was wary of alcohol, in her weakened state.

Although it was very ordinary wine – Graham would have refused to drink it – the cold green taste of each mouthful was heady and transforming, worth whatever it would cost her afterwards. She began to feel liberated and exhilarated, just as she might have felt when she was twenty. It occurred to her – but very calmly, the way

176

you might describe a limb getting over an attack of pins and needles – that she was coming back to life. And yet all her attention was focused on what was in the newspaper, not on herself. She understood that her own experience was a tiny atom beside the cold, hard masses of history and politics, full of cruel truths. Boyd had read to her, the other night, about the men who had died cutting or tunnelling through the rock to build those early railways: killed in explosions or by runaway wagons, or crushed by falling stones, or by the buckets that carried the stone – and the men – up and down in the shafts. Twenty-six were killed, to make one tunnel.

She didn't look at her watch again until two twenty: it was surely too late now for any meeting in the Palm House. Then, glancing out of the café window, she actually saw the young man from the train walking purposefully along the street, away from the park. So he had turned up; Greta had begun not to believe in the meeting, thinking she must have misheard him. This proof of his independent, real existence was dismaying, because he'd come to seem a figment of her fantasy: in her memory she had smoothed him out, forgetting that in his looks there was something unsettling and blatant – the thick lashes and coarse skin and big, sensuous mouth were in excess of any personality he'd shown her. His expression was intent and preoccupied; he wore his white mac and was still carrying his briefcase, and she was jolted by a pang of guilt for his loneliness. As he passed close by the cafe window, she tapped on the glass to attract his attention. Looking around, he was startled and forlorn. She had caught him out in his desolation: they were strangers to each other; he might even be angry with her because she'd let him down.

Smiling, placatory, Greta beckoned him inside. As soon as he recognised her, she saw him smother the raw truth she'd glimpsed, preparing his bright face for her approval like a good boy. While he made his way towards her – rattling at the wrong door first, which didn't open – she was already regretting the loss of her solitude. He looked out of place in the hippie bar: he had even put on a tie under the maroon jumper, perhaps in her honour. She wanted to buy him a drink in return for the coffee at the station, but he insisted that he'd never let a lady pay for anything, and it wasn't worth arguing with him. He bought himself a Coke and got her another glass of wine, though she'd said she didn't want one, and really didn't. Still, once the wine was in front of her she couldn't help taking swallows of it, just to ease the awkwardness of the situation. He didn't mention that she hadn't turned up to meet him. In fact, he said he was so glad she'd come, as if the bar had been their plan all along; counting his change carefully, he put it away in a little purse in the pocket of his mac.

— I knew you were an easy person to get on with, he said. — As soon as I saw you.

— I'm not really very easy. You don't know me at all.

He insisted that he was a good judge of people, he could always tell. Then they exchanged names: he was Mitchell, and she explained that she was Greta, short for

Margaret. Astonished and delighted, he said that Margaret was his mother's name. — You see, it's funny because I had this feeling, before you even told me. I just knew what you were going to say. Greta wasn't sure that she believed in this coincidence, although it would be a strange thing for him to lie about. She remembered the impression she'd had on the train, that he was a chameleon making himself up to fit into any circumstances – to please her, or so that he could appear competent and connected. The wine was making her dizzy. — Kate's father persuaded me to change my name to Greta, she said. — Even before Mrs Thatcher, he hated Margaret.

— Are you divorced?

She explained that Ian had died in an accident, long ago. — Though we weren't together by then, anyway. And I've been married for years to someone else.

— But I suppose Kate's father was the love of your life.

Greta was aware of laughing too loudly, and thought people were looking at them. They might imagine that Mitchell was her son or her nephew. Or they might detect something fervid and artificial in her reactions to him, and wonder whether he was a con man tricking her out of her money, or a gigolo she was paying for. She said she didn't believe in that kind of love. It turned out that Mitchell believed not only in true love but also in destiny. Certain individuals were fated to be together. Everything that happened had its purpose, he said, even if we couldn't see it. Yet, all the time he was setting out these platitudes with such solemnity, Greta felt sure that they weren't the real content of his thoughts, just as her own sceptical, condescending cleverness when she argued with him wasn't the real content of her thoughts either. This conversation took place on the surface, while their real lives were hidden underground beneath it, crouching, listening out, mutely attentive. Mitchell's physical reality was like a third presence at the table: his bitten skin and slanted, suffering cheekbones.

— I brought something for you, he said. — It's a present.

Greta protested anxiously that she didn't want any present, but he ignored her and twiddled with the combination lock on his briefcase, then lifted the lid importantly and took out a thick paperback book, well read, its pages furry with use. Judging by the cover illustration and the title in embossed gold letters, it was the kind of historical novel Greta wouldn't dream of reading: a gritty, working-class romance, all arrogant mill owners and salt-of-the-earth girls in shawls and clogs.

— I don't want it, she said. — I hardly know you.

— Please. I want you to have it. I know you'll enjoy it.

Thrusting the book at her, he managed somehow to knock over his drink; sticky Coke ran down the edge of the table and onto her skirt, though she shoved herself smartly backwards in her chair. She had thought he was just drinking Coke, but she could smell now that there was alcohol in it, too, something sweet and strong – rum, perhaps.

— Oh, Jesus! Mitchell said. — Jesus, I'm so sorry.

— It doesn't matter. Don't make a fuss.

While Greta rummaged for a packet of tissues in her handbag, Mitchell ran to the bar for paper napkins. When he came back he knelt on the floor in front of her, dabbing at the wet patch on her skirt. — Will the stain come out? he said.

— Don't fuss. It's nothing, honestly. It won't stain.

Their table was in a little nook beside the window, so that he wasn't easily visible to the other customers. Suddenly he dropped his head into her lap, face down between her thighs. It was so unexpected, and his head weighed so heavily, that at first Greta thought he must have passed out. She could feel the heat of his breath through the wet cloth. She pushed at his head, not liking the feel of the coarse wire of his hair in her hands.

— Get off me, she said urgently and quietly, not wanting to draw anyone's attention. — Get up right now.

He lifted his head and looked at her blearily, as if he hardly saw her, as if she'd roused him out of sleep.

— Leave me alone, she said.

— I'm sorry. I'm really sorry.

— You'd better go. You're making a spectacle of yourself.

Obediently, he got to his feet then, and he grabbed at his mac and briefcase and headed to the wrong door again, tugging desperately at the handle. Greta wouldn't look up to see him go; she was burning with humiliation, exposed to all the customers in the cafe. He had left his book on the table and she opened it, just so that she

181

didn't have to see whether anyone was watching. A business card was tucked inside the front cover, with Mitchell's name printed on it, and the name of the company he worked for. His phone number was circled in biro. And there, written on the flyleaf of the book, was her name. *To Margaret*, it said. *With love.* Greta was confused, and for one long moment she really believed that it was fated, that this stranger had known her before he ever met her, and that he had written her name inside his book before she even told him what it was.

Her Share of Sorrow

Ruby's mother, Dalia, used to be a dancer before she had her children. Then she'd trained to be a psychotherapist, and you got the feeling she'd disowned her dancing days, looking back on them as delusion and vanity. Yet still she carried herself in that dancer's exquisitely conscious way, as if she was held taut by a thread running up from the crown of her head; she was still hollowly thin, and painted her eyes with black upward-swept lines, and wore her hair pulled back austerely from the sculpted bones of her face. Serious psychotherapist glasses added intellectual distinction to Dalia's other graces.

Ruby's name might have suited her if she'd been smouldering and mysterious like her mother in the dance photographs. But she was plump and stubby with short fat arms, lank beige-colour hair, and fair freckled skin that turned pink easily in the sun or if she told lies – which she quite often did. She looked like a changeling in that family, other people thought – because Ruby's older brother Nico and her father Adrian, administrator for an innovative theatre company, were also distinguished and beautiful and tall like Dalia, and very thin. Scrupulously, because they'd read all the right guides to parenting, Adrian and Dalia ignored Ruby's greedy eating at the supper table. They never had cake or ice cream in the house, but she raided the cupboards and stole money to buy sweets; there was always a mess of crumbs and wrappers on the floor around where she sat playing on her computer. Each evening Dalia arrived in her daughter's bedroom, strained and full of reasoned explanation, to enforce their rule that Ruby was only supposed to have computer-time for an hour; this resulted in stormy sessions of weeping, on both their parts. Lying on her back on her Spider-Man duvet, Ruby wailed at the ceiling, her small mouth stretched open in an ugly shape, her face hot-pink. — What am I supposed to *do*? she lamented. — There's nothing for me to *do* in this house!

— But she isn't interested in anything! Dalia, also lamenting, wailed to her husband. — She doesn't draw, she doesn't read, she doesn't play imaginative games. She's not even sporty; she can't swim. And she isn't finding out information on the wretched computer, she's just looking at pictures of kittens in wellington boots or playing Crossy Road or messaging her friends. Not that she's got any friends.

— That's not fair, Adrian reproached his wife gently. — She does have friends.

— Yes, but such hopeless ones.

Dalia remembered taking Nico to an exhibition of Greek art when he was much younger than Ruby was now. She had loved watching him as he'd dwelled on each momentous sculpture, huge eyes drinking it in; then he'd read the accompanying information absorbedly, running his finger along under the words on the plaques. Now Nico had a place to do PPE at Oxford, and was a gifted cellist. Needless to say Ruby's fingers wouldn't even work to cover the holes on the recorder. Her parents had gone to great lengths to get her into a good school where she might be stimulated; she had a lovely teacher, a real high-flyer who kept a separate spreadsheet on her phone for each of the children in her class, making a note whenever they learned anything new. At parents' evenings this teacher was brightly hopeful about Ruby, who sat stolidly somewhere in the middle of her attainment targets.

Ruby was ten years old when they borrowed a house in the South of France from friends, for three weeks in the summer. Adrian and Nico hired bikes and were out all day. Dalia needed desperately to unwind and leave her clients behind; she took her book out into the garden, where an apricot tree was trained against a crumbling brick wall and flower beds were edged with lavender – bracing herself for conflict with Ruby, who couldn't live without Wi-Fi and hated the sun. She came out scowling into the brightness, stomping her feet in her jelly shoes. Hopefully Dalia suggested she should go exploring. – This is a fascinating old place, she said. – It belonged to the Williamses' parents, they've been coming here forever. There are all kinds of treasures in the outhouses.

— But I don't care about the Williamses, Ruby said.

Dalia closed her eyes and after a pause the jelly shoes stomped indoors again.

Then things went rather quiet inside the house. Dalia fell asleep in the healing warmth, under the shade of the faded striped umbrella, and when she woke up an hour later and everything was still quiet she felt afraid. Stepping indoors, where the shutters were barred against the blazing day, she was blind at first in the shadows. Ruby wasn't anywhere to be found downstairs, or on the first floor. Dalia climbed the steep uncarpeted steps to the attic, which the Williamses only used to store old junk; the heat up here under the roof was feral, dizzy-making. Some furtive noise from behind the closed attic door, a small scratching or rustling, made her hesitate outside it.

— Ruby, are you in there? Are you all right?

— I'm fine, thank you.

There was something peculiar about Ruby's voice, prim and slippery and secretive; for all her professional openness to things sexual, Dalia shied away from opening the door, afraid of what might be on the other side. — All right, darling, just so long as you're OK.

Ruby spent all day in the attic, with only a break for baguette, and appeared downstairs chastely enough, though hot-faced, at supper time; she ate without commenting on the food and as soon as the meal was finished slipped upstairs again. — I'm just doing something, she said, avoiding eye contact. The three left behind in peace, to play chess or read or make music – there was a passable piano for Adrian, and Nico had brought his cello – looked at one another in amused perplexity.

— You know what she's doing, don't you? Adrian said later, coming down from visiting the bathroom.

— Do I want to know?

— She's just reading.

— Reading? Really?

— I opened the door a crack and peeked inside and she didn't even hear me. Just sitting there sucking her hair, completely lost inside her book, although it's still boiling up there under the roof.

— What book? She didn't bring any books.

At ten o'clock they had to call Ruby down to go to bed; when she was asleep they tried the attic door, but found that she had locked it and hidden the key. The next day after breakfast she slipped inconspicuously upstairs again. Nico followed her up to the attic – though finely sensitive, he was not above teasing his exasperating sister – and found this time she'd locked the door on the inside. Dalia did feel vaguely guilty. Who knew what books Ruby had stumbled upon? They might be pornography; or sinister old medical textbooks. The Williamses were rather awful. But the peace in the quiet house was blissful, and she was soon addicted to her quiet hours alone in the walled garden.

Behind the locked door Ruby was already three-quarters of the way through *East Lynne*. This was only one volume in a promisingly tall pile of Treasury Classics – *The Woman in White*, *The Cloister and the Hearth*, *Ivanhoe*, *Lady Audley's Secret* – uniformly bound in red with gold lettering. The younger generation of Williamses had moved them up here to make room on their shelves for something slightly less dated; they bought the Booker shortlist every year, and the backlist was overspilling their London home. When Ruby first strayed into the attic, she had opened the volume on the top of the pile in a spirit of despairing mockery, because she'd never in the least liked books before. The ones she'd been given as presents, or been forced to read in class, had seemed too drearily like her own real-life childish routines of home and school and family. She hadn't had any idea that books could transport you like this – into something better.

At night, falling asleep, she snuffed up the fragrance of damp-spotted old pages on her fingers; in the mornings she hurried through her chocolate milk and croissant, hungry to get back to her story. Much of *East Lynne*, in truth, was fairly incomprehensible; she stumbled among strange facts in a thick fog. The prohibitions that weighed so heavily on Lady Isabel Vane and Sir Francis Levison – what *had* they done wrong exactly? – were all the more compelling for their obscurity; some grandeur in the language intoxicated her. She was astonished when little William died. Children always got better in books, didn't they? '*I have seen the flowers we shall see in Heaven,*' he said, '*ten times brighter than our flowers here. When*

God takes a little child there it is because he loves him.' The audacity of it took Ruby's breath away, as if something raw and wild had been dragged from where it was concealed, into the daylight. Tears flooded into her eyes; what was inside her seemed poured out onto the page.

'I have had more than my share of sorrow,' Madame Vine said. *'Sometimes I think that I cannot support it.'* When day faded in the attic Ruby went on reading by torchlight, and when at last she had to go to bed, she placed her silken bookmark with trembling fingers. She staggered up dazedly from the world of her story, as if the one she returned to were the insubstantial fiction.

By the end of their holiday she had read *East Lynne* and *The Heir of Redclyffe*, and was a good way into *Lady Audley's Secret.* Now she would never find out what the secret was. Although it was searing to be torn away from her book, Ruby never dreamed of carrying it off with her; it would have been a desecration, to steal one volume from where it belonged among its fellows. Anyway, she liked to think of it left behind in the attic empty without her, somnolent in the sunshine, lizards basking on the stone windowsill outside, motionless as stone itself. At home in Crouch End it didn't occur to her – she wasn't resourceful – that she could have got hold of *Lady Audley* easily enough, in a library or online. She couldn't ask her parents or her brother for help because she was afraid of letting them in on her reading discoveries in case they somehow appropriated them, turning out to know already all about the Williamses' wonderful books. Ruby clung on to an indistinct idea, in fact, that the copy of *Lady Audley* she'd read was the only copy, the single exemplar, unique in the world. Fatalistically she accepted its loss, and her days were bitter with the flavour of exile from her whole self.

There were two weeks of holiday left before she returned to school; she went on play-dates with friends, was taken to see *Shaun the Sheep*, and went back to quarrelling with Dalia: but all this listlessly, as if her heart wasn't in it. Then during one dull rainy afternoon, while her mother had sessions with clients and Nico was supposed to be looking after her, but was browsing his laptop on the sofa, Ruby was filled from one moment to the next with a vision of possibility. All its elements – the possession of the right virgin notebook, a picture of her own head bowed in rapt concentration over her page, the shape of her story – came together in a single lightning-strike of inspiration.

— Where are you off to, Pud? Nico said without looking up. – No going anywhere near Mama, you know that.

— Just had a thought, said Ruby innocently.

— A thought? You're kidding me.

Her parents were delighted with whatever was keeping Ruby quiet in her bedroom; they supposed she had resumed the reading she'd begun in France. In fact she'd only glanced briefly inside the old unloved books on her shelf at home, whose ordinary reality was flavourless as ever. But she'd found something to do that matched or even outdid the thrill of her French books – and one evening her joy in her day's creation overflowed her caution. She announced to her family that she was writing a novel.

— Darling, that's wonderful! said Dalia with real warmth. — How interesting!

Adrian, beaming, said that he'd always thought she might have a novelist in her.

— You could show it to your new class teacher, Dalia said. — What's it about?

Already Ruby was regretting telling them. — Things, she said insouciantly.

They couldn't have been more enthusiastic; Adrian promised that when she was finished he'd show it to a friend who was a publisher. Yet oddly even in their enthusiasm there was something tainting and disappointing – perhaps because no amount of it could ever match the power and importance Ruby felt when she was making things up. Sucking her hair, biro squeezed in her clutching fat fingers, joining up her letters laboriously, she transcribed the scenes unfolding in her mind's eye; her whole body, kneeling up on her chair, hunched over her notebook, seemed shaken by their intensity. Sometimes she spoke the words she wrote aloud, or acted them out with a scowl or disdainful toss of her head.

Her family professed great interest in reading her novel but she held back, with uncharacteristic restraint; something delicate in her story needed her protection.

Carefully, whenever she finished writing, she stowed her notebook away under the mattress on her bed. But one late afternoon, in a careless moment between chapters, she left it lying on her desk while she foraged in the stash of biscuits in her wardrobe. Nico, peering in from the room next door, where he was marking time uneasily before Balliol, swooped on it.

Ruby ran screaming downstairs after him, to where their parents were making salad in the kitchen. — Dad, he's got my novel! He's stolen it!

— Nico, that's not on.

— No, no, really, it's brilliant, Nico said, laughing, holding it out of Ruby's way where she was jumping up at him, trying to snatch at it.

— It's unforgivable, Nico, Dalia said, pausing sternly with an organic tomato in one hand and a knife in the other. — Give it back to her right now.

— Listen, let me read you some of this. You won't believe it. *Lady Carole, her cheek pale as a dove's wing, swept from the ballroom with a flash of her exquisite eyes, dragging her long amber curls behind her.* Do you think she's taken off her wig? Meanwhile *Frederick Fillet gazed into the dying coals* – coals spelled c-o-l-e-s – *of the fire.*

— I like the sound of Frederick Fillet, Adrian said. — Is he our hero?

Ruby knew this was all a disaster and yet, succumbing to a writer's vanity, she couldn't help half wanting to hear her words take on their own life in the world. Her eyes were fixed on Nico, pleading but also with a greedy

192

curiosity. What did she sound like, really? Wouldn't they be amazed? Wouldn't the words forged in such passion stupefy her audience, making them at last see what she saw? She mouthed over silently what Nico was reading out loud.

— *'But,' stuttered Lady Carole, dread seeping into her. 'Surely you are not the one who once betrayed me and ran off with another woman?' The cords of her life were snapping. 'It cannot be.' Frederick sobbed, laying his rugged head upon her breasts. 'Forgive me, you are much more beautiful than she is.'*

— Upon her breasts, Adrian said. — My word.

— *'I do not reproach you,' Lady Carole said. 'Because really she is quite nice.'*

Ruby spun round on her parents, riven suddenly with suspicion. Adrian was grinning helplessly; the back of Dalia's hand, still clutching the vegetable knife, was pressed against her mouth, and her eyes behind her glasses seemed to be staring in distress – for a moment Ruby believed her mother was ravaged by the emotion in the story. Then she saw that her shoulders were shaking.

— What are you all laughing at? she shouted furiously. — Why is it funny?

She stayed barricaded and inconsolable in her room that evening, though they all came humbly with apologies, and left propitiatory presents, even chocolate. — I'm very, very angry with Nico, Dalia communicated through the closed door. — It was very wrong of him. We didn't

193

really think your story was funny, darling. We were just laughing with . . .

Ruby heard her search for the right word.

— With delight, that's all.

Ruby had her notebook back and was writing in it again. At first she worked bitterly and without conviction. They had hollowed out the best thing she'd ever done: she would finish the stupid story any old how, just to prove they were right, and what an idiot she was. As time passed, however, the work regained its hold over her – and the plot altered unexpectedly from her original idea. Outside her bedroom window it grew dark, and the ordinary landscape of smart back gardens and pergolas and trampolines receded; an extraordinary huge moon, the colour of yellow cream, rose into the turquoise sky and seemed to be dissolving into an aureole of light around its rim. A mysterious wasting fever struck down all the members of Lady Carole's family and also Frederick Fillet, one by one. Lady Carole never slept, but moved between their bedsides holding up a lamp, putting precious drops of water to their lips and wiping their brows with paper tissues. All in vain. *'Oh, but it is hard to part,'* they murmured. By the time Ruby had finished – on the last line of the last page in her notebook, as she'd always planned – they had all passed beyond that river from whose bourne there is no known return, and Lady Carole was left alone. Ruby dropped tears on her page for her dear family. Her heart was swollen with love, and writerly triumph.

Silk Brocade

Ann Gallagher was listening to the wireless, cutting out a boxy short jacket with three-quarter-length sleeves, in a pale lilac wool flecked with navy. She had cut the pattern from her own design – there was a matching knee-length pencil skirt – then pinned the paper shapes onto the length of cloth, arranging and rearranging them like pieces of a puzzle to make them fit with minimum waste. Now her scissors bit in with finality, growling against the wood surface of the table, the cloth falling away cleanly from the blades. These scissors were sacrosanct and deadly, never to be used on anything that might blunt them. Ann and her friend Kit Seaton were renting the back basement of a big house in a residential area of Bristol for their dressmaking business; because the house was built on a hill, their rooms opened onto a garden, and sunlight fell through the French windows in shifting patches onto Ann's cutting table.

Someone came down the steps to the side entrance, then tapped on the opaque glass panes of the door; Ann

195

looked up, irritated at being interrupted. Kit said they should always switch over to the Third Programme when clients came – it was more sophisticated – but there wasn't time, and Ann could make out enough through the bubbled glass to know that the woman standing on the other side wasn't sophisticated anyway. She was too bulky, planted there too stolidly, with an unassuming patience. Some clients pushed their faces up against the door and rattled the handle if they were kept waiting for even a moment.

– Ann? Do you remember me? It's Nola.

Nola Higgins stood with military straightness, shoulders squared; she was buttoned up into some sort of navy-blue uniform, unflatteringly tight over her heavy bust. – I know I shouldn't have turned up without an appointment, she apologised cheerfully. – But do you mind if I ask a quick question?

Ann and Nola had grown up in the same street in Fishponds and had both won bursary places at the same girls' grammar school. Nola was already in her third year when Ann started, but Ann had ignored her overtures of friendship and avoided sitting next to her on the bus that took them home. She'd hoped that Nola understood about her need to make new friends and leave Fishponds behind. Nola had trained to be a district nurse when she left school, and Ann didn't often cross paths with her; now she guessed, with a sinking heart, that Nola had come to ask her to make her wedding dress. There had been other girls from her Fishponds past who'd wanted her to do this – it wasn't strictly speaking even

196

her past, because for the moment she was still living there, at home with her family. She and Kit needed the work, but Kit said that if they were seen to be sewing for just anyone they'd never get off the ground with the right people. Perhaps when Nola knew their prices she'd be put off. Hesitating, Ann looked at her wristwatch. — Look, why don't you come on in for ten minutes? I am busy, but I'll take a break. I'll put some coffee on to perk.

She showed Nola into the fitting room. They had a sewing room and a fitting room and a little windowless kitchenette and a lavatory; a dentist on the ground floor used the front basement rooms for storage, and they sometimes heard his heavy footsteps on the stairs. The Third Programme helped drown out the sound of his drill when clients came for fittings. Ann and Kit had made gold velvet curtains for the fitting-room windows and covered a chaise longue in matching velvet; on the white walls there were prints of paintings by Klee and Utrillo and a gilt antique mirror with a plant trailing round it. Morning light waited, importantly empty, in the cheval glass. Kit sometimes brought her boyfriends to this room at night, and Ann had to be on the lookout for the telltale signs – dirty ashtrays, wine glasses, crumpled cushions. She was convinced that Kit had actually been making love once on top of someone's evening dress, laid out on the chaise longue after a fitting.

Ann wondered whether Nola Higgins was impressed by the glamorous new style of her life or simply accepted it, as calmly as she'd have accepted any place she walked into. She must have seen some things during the course

197

of her work as a nurse, some of them horrors. Nola's home perm made her look closer to their mothers' age; the dark curls were too tight and flat against her head, and when she sat down she tugged her skirt over her knees, self-conscious about her broad hips. But her brown eyes were very alert and steady, and she had that kind of skin that was so soft it looked almost loose on her bones, matte pink as if she were wearing powder, though she wasn't.

Ann put on the percolator in the kitchenette. Kit had grown up in France, or claimed she had, and insisted that they always make real coffee. They served it in little turquoise coffee cups, with bitter-almond biscuits, on a Japanese lacquer tray that Ann had found in a junk shop. Sometimes the coffee was so strong the clients could hardly swallow it.

— I won't keep you long, Nola said. — But I have a favour to ask.

She didn't have the same broad Bristol accent as her parents – Ann's mother would have said that she was nicely spoken. It was about a wedding dress, of course. The wedding would be in June, Nola said. It would be a quiet one, at least she hoped so. She knew this was short notice and probably Ann was all booked up, but they had decided in a hurry. — Not that kind of hurry, she added, laughing without embarrassment. — I suppose you sometimes have to let out the waists as the brides get bigger.

Ann was accomplished at congratulating other women on their engagements. She hardly felt a pang – felt instead something sprightly and audacious, more like relief. — Do you know about our prices? she said tactfully. — I could show you a price list.

— Oh, that won't be a problem, Nola began to say. — Because the man I'm marrying, my fiancé –

And then she had to break off, because her eyes brimmed with tears and a red heat came into her cheeks; Ann had an intuition that the flush ran thrillingly all over her body. Who'd have thought that Nola Higgins would be susceptible to that kind of thrill? She was bending over her handbag, fishing for a handkerchief. — How silly, she said. — It's ridiculous, Ann. But I'm just so happy. I can't quite believe that I'm saying those words, that we're really going to be married. He's such a lovely chap. And he'll be able to pay your prices. I knew you wouldn't be cheap.

— Aren't you the lucky one, Ann admired. — A lovely chap, and he can pay as well!

— I am lucky! Don't I know it. I was his nurse, you know, when he was very poorly. That's how we met. But it's not how it sounds: that isn't what he wants me for, just to look after him. I mean, to see him now you couldn't tell he was ever ill, except he has a little limp, that's all.

— I'm happy for you, Ann said.

Nola sat very still, holding up her coffee cup in both hands, smiling almost dazedly, accepting the tribute. She had brought some fabric with her in a paper bag – the brides often did, and Ann usually had to talk them out of it. Her fiancé had a lot of material in his home, Nola said, put away in trunks and cupboards. And there were some

lovely old clothes too: Ann should come out and see sometime. Ann made a politely interested noise, wondering if
he kept a second-hand shop; she was imagining someone
much older than Nola, respectable and considerate, quiet,
perhaps a widower. The material in the bag smelled of
mothballs but it looked expensive – thick silk brocade, off-
white, embroidered with cream flowers. — It's old, Nola
said, but it's never been used. And there's some lace too,
good lace. I didn't bring that – I wanted to ask you first.

She fingered the brocade uneasily, staring down at
it. — It's too much, isn't it? I'll look like a dog's dinner,
that's what I said. I just want to wear something sensible,
look like myself. But he insisted, said I had to bring it.

Ann really was convinced that if only you could find
the right clothes you could become whatever you wanted,
you could transform yourself. She let the heavy fabric fall
out of its folds and made Nola stand up, then held it against
her in front of the cheval mirror, pulling it in around her
waist, frowning expertly at Nola's reflection across her
shoulder, tugging and smoothing the cloth as if she were
moulding something. — You see? The rich off-white is
very flattering against your dark hair and your lovely skin.
There isn't enough for a whole dress if you want full-length,
but I think we could get a fitted bodice and a little peplum
out of it and find a matching plain fabric for the skirt. With
your full figure you want to go for a nice clean silhouette,
nothing fussy. This could look stunning, actually.

— Do you think so? Nola's eyes, doubting and
trusting, looked out from the reflection into hers.

*　*　*

Kit came slamming through the glass door after lunch, in the middle of telling some crazy story, screaming with laughter, half cut already, with a couple of men friends in tow. Ann was just starting on the lining for the lilac suit. One of the friends was a medic, Ray, Kit's current boyfriend, or he thought he was – Ann knew about other things, one married man in particular. The second friend was also a medic. Ann hadn't seen him before: Donny Ross, who played the piano, apparently, in a jazz band. Donny Ross had a body as thin as a whip and cavernous cheeks and thick jet-black hair with a long quiff that flopped into his eyes. His mouth was small and his grin was surprisingly girlish, showing his small teeth, though he didn't grin much – or say much. He was mostly saturnine and judgemental. It was obvious to Ann right away that Donny didn't think much of Kit. He saw through her bossy know-how and the whole parade of her snobbery: going on about how Proust was her favourite author and her mother used to have her hats made in the Champs-Elysées and weren't the little bureaucrats who wanted our taxes so ghastly – as if she couldn't guess what Ann had guessed already, that Donny was a socialist.

He got up while Kit was still talking and went into the kitchenette, banging through the cupboards, looking for something he didn't find – alcohol, probably; he came out with the bag of sugar and a cup of the coffee that Ann had made for Nola earlier, which must have been quite cold. Then he sat spooning sugar out of the bag into his cup, no saucer, spilling it all over the table, six or seven spoonfuls just to make the coffee bearable, and Kit didn't say a word about the sugar bag, though she was so particular about everything being served up in the right way. Perhaps Donny Ross frightened her, Ann thought.

She told Kit about Nola's wedding then; best to get it over with while she was in this mood, and there was company. — I know it's not exactly our style, she said. — But we could do with the work.

She gave Kit the piece of paper where Nola had written down the details, and expected her to make her usual disdainful face when she read through it, as if something smelled funny. Kit had a long, horsey face, tousled honey-coloured hair, and a stubby, sexy, decisive little body, like an overdeveloped child's; she expressed all her tastes and distastes as if they afflicted her physically, through her senses. To Ann's surprise, she sat up excitedly. — Oh Lawd, this is a marvel. I can't believe you don't know where this wedding is, you angel-innocent. It's the most perfect little bijou Queen Anne house, tucked away into its own deer park on the way to Bath. Look what you've done, you clever daft thing! The pictures will be in all the good papers.

— But Nola Higgins is from Fishponds. We were at school together.

— I don't care who she is. She's marrying a Perney, and they've owned Thwaite Park for centuries.

Then Ann began to understand why Nola thought she was so lucky. She explained it all to Kit, and showed her the old brocade that Nola had left. — She said he had lots more fabric in his house. And old clothes too – she thought I might like to see them. And I turned her down! I thought he must be running some kind of second-hand shop!

— Which, in a funny way, you could say he was, said Donny Ross.

Kit flopped back onto the chaise longue in exaggerated despair, limbs flung out like a doll's. — When she comes back, you're to tell her you've changed your mind. I'd die for an invitation to go out there and poke around. Imagine what they've got in their attic!

— Skeletons, Donny Ross said.

Later that afternoon, while Kit put on different outfits to entertain Ray – and at some point Ray exhibited himself too, in a green satin gown, made up with Kit's lipstick and powder – Donny Ross came prowling around where Ann was cutting out the lining for the suit. — Do you mind? he said. And he called her an angel-innocent and a clever daft thing, in a comical, mincing, falsetto voice. Ann didn't usually let people into the sewing room; she was anxious about keeping the fabrics pristine. With his hands in his pockets, frowning, Donny was working through some jazz tune to himself, in a way you couldn't really call singing; it was more as if he were imitating all the different instruments in turn, taking his hands out of his pockets to bang out the drum part on the end of her cutting table. Ann might just as well not have been there: he threw his head back and stared up into the corners of the room as if all the evidence of her sewing, spread out around him, was simply too frivolous for him to look at. It was peculiar that she didn't feel any urge to entertain or charm him, though she knew how charming she could be when she tried. She carried on steadily, concentrating on her work. Some new excitement seemed to be waiting, folded up inside her, not even tried on yet.

Nola met Kit when she dropped in to look at Ann's designs. She was still wearing her nurse's uniform; she wanted to keep on working until she married. Kit went all out to win her over and Nola sat blinking and smiling – her plain black shoes planted together on the floor, her back straight – under the assault of Kit's crazy exuberance, her flattery. Kit really was good fun; when you were with her something new and outrageous could happen at any moment. Going through the drawings, Nola was full of trepidation. The models in Ann's designs were haughty and impossibly slender, drifting with their noses tipped up disdainfully. This was how she'd learned to draw them at art college; it was only a kind of shorthand, an aspiration. If you knew how to read the designs, they gave all the essential information about seams and darts.

— She knows what she's doing, Kit reassured Nola. — She's a genius.

Kit sewed well, and she had a good eye for style; she could work hard when she put her mind to it, but she couldn't design for toffee or cut a pattern. — Ann's going to make my fortune for me, she said. — You wait until we move the business up to London. We'll be dressing all the stars of stage and screen. I'd put my life in her hands.

— These do look beautiful, Nola conceded yearningly.

Eventually they decided on something classic, full-length, very simple, skimming Nola's figure without hugging it. Ann would use the brocade Nola had brought for the bodice and the sleeves, and a matching silk satin, if they could find it, for the skirt. — Unless there's any more of the brocade?

Of course they'd planned all along to ask her this, angling for an invitation to Thwaite Park. And eagerly Nola invited them. — Blaise would love to meet you, she said. Privately, Kit chose to doubt this. — He probably thinks it's pretty funny, she said, — being invited to meet his fiancée's dressmaker. I mean, their love affair's the most darling romantic story I've ever heard, and Nola's an angel – but what I wouldn't give to be a fly on the wall at that wedding! Fishponds meets Thwaite Park.

— What do you know about Fishponds? Ann said sharply.

— Come on, Annie-Pannie. You think it's pretty extraordinary too, I know you do. Don't be chippy, don't get on your old socialist high horse, just because you've got a pash on Mr Misery-Guts Donny Ross.

So Kit and Ann drove out one Sunday, with Ray and Donny Ross, for a picnic at Thwaite Park. Kit was engaged to Ray by this time, though Ann didn't take that too seriously. She'd been engaged several times already; and anyway Ann knew the other thing was still going on with Kit's married man, Charlie, who was a lawyer. Ann had bumped into Charlie recently, out shopping with his wife and children. She'd been waltzing around the fitting room with him only the night before, while Kit played Edith Piaf on the portable Black Box gramophone he'd bought her, yet when he passed her in the street he pretended not to know her, staring at her blankly. His wife was hanging onto his arm, and Charlie held his gloves in his clasped hands behind his back; as Ann looked after them, he waggled his free fingers at her in a jaunty, naughty secret signal.

On the day of the picnic it was warm for the first time since winter and the clear air was as heady as spirits. Ray put down the roof on his convertible and drove fast. Kit tied on a headscarf, but Ann hadn't thought to bring one, so her hair whipped in her face, and by the time they turned in between the crumbling stone gateposts – there were no gates; they must have been requisitioned for the war effort – she was bewildered with the speed and the rushing air. The house was a Palladian box, perfectly proportioned, understated to the point of plainness, its blonde stone blackened with soot; sooty sheep grazed on a long meadow sloping down in front of it. A few skinny lambs scampered under the ancient oaks, where new leaves were just beginning to spring out, implausibly, from the grey crusty limbs. There were other cars in the drive and in the car park, because the house and grounds were open to the public. Laughing and talking confidently – at least, Kit was laughing and confident – they walked right past the main entrance, where tickets were on sale; peacocks were shrieking and displaying on the stable wall. Nola had instructed them to come round the side of the house, then press the bell beside a door marked 'Private' in white painted letters. Ann half expected a butler. Donny was stiff with disapproval of class privilege.

Blaise Perney – who opened the side door himself, promptly, as if he'd been waiting for them – wasn't in the least what they'd prepared for. To begin with, he looked younger than Nola: very tall and ugly, diffident and smiling and stooped, with a long bony face and hair like crinkled pale silk. He welcomed them effusively, blushing as if they were doing him a favour, and said that he was so looking forward to getting to know them. Ann thought with relief that Blaise could easily be won over; she always made this assessment, when she first met men, of whether or not she could get round them if she chose to test her power. Charlie, for instance – although he liked her and flirted with her madly – she could never have deflected from his own path in a million years, whereas Ray was a walkover. Blaise said that Nola was packing a picnic in the kitchen. He led them through a succession of shadowy, chilly, gracious rooms with shuttered windows, apologising for the mess and the state of decay: his dragging foot seemed to be part of his diffidence.

These were private rooms, not open to the public, not arranged to look like scenes from the past but with the past and present simply jumbled together: a cheap little wireless set balanced on a pile of leather-bound books, a milkman's calendar among the silver-framed photos on a desk whose roll-top was broken, an ordinary electric fire in a huge marble fireplace dirty with wood ash. Ann found this much more romantic; it set her imagination racing. What she could have done with this place if it were hers! In the cavernous, dark kitchen, where the giant-sized iron range was cold and there were fifty dinner plates in a wooden rack, Nola in a summer dress was boiling eggs on a Baby Belling, looking surprisingly at home. Ann's envy was only fleeting – it was benevolent, gracious. Whatever lay ahead for her, she thought, was better than any house.

When they took their picnic outside, Blaise said that they should have seen the gardens when his mother was alive. Nola in her funny, shapeless flowery dress, squinting and smiling into the sun, looked more like a mother than anyone's wife; they saw how she would restore things and bring back order. Scrambling up among birch trees in a little wood, they were out of the way of the visitors on the paths below; the bluebells were like pools of water among the trees, reflecting the sky. Ray and Donny raced like schoolboys and wrestled each other to the ground, while Kit kept up her bubbling talk, making it sound to Blaise as if she and Ann were specialists in old fabrics. Hoping for more brocade, she said, they hadn't started yet on Nola's dress. Blaise said they must go in search of the brocade later. There were all sorts of old clothes and fabrics and embroideries upstairs in the cedarwood presses, he told them; he'd hardly looked in there himself but would love them to discover something valuable, which he could sell. — You can help yourself to anything you like. I expect it's all old junk. I'll show you around properly when the public have gone. Not that I'm objecting to the public, because they are my bread and butter.

— What happened to your leg, old man? Ray asked.

Blaise apologised, because he wasn't a war hero. He'd managed to catch the dreaded polio – wasn't that childish of him? Nola spread out a tablecloth in a little hollow among the bluebells, while the young doctors interrogated her sternly about neck stiffness, light intolerance, respiratory muscle weakness. Blaise rolled up his trouser leg and Ray and Donny examined his twisted, skinny calf; Kit turned her face away, because she didn't like looking at sickness or deformed things. Yet Blaise Perney was hardly deformed at all; he'd made a wonderful recovery. He told them that Nola had saved his life, and she laughed with shy pleasure. She said he was just lucky, that was all.

The surprise was that Blaise turned out to be as much of a socialist as Donny Ross, even if he did own a deer park. He didn't object to any of the taxes, he said. The only damn problem was finding enough money to pay them, because old houses these days didn't come with money attached. Thwaite was a bottomless pit when it came to money. He ought to give the place up, sell it for a hotel or something, but he was too sentimental. Anyway, there were an awful lot of big old houses on the market, and it wasn't a good time in the hotel business. He and Nola called each other 'dear' and passed each other salt, in a twist of greaseproof paper, to go with the eggs. Kit had made little crustless sandwiches with cucumber and foie gras from a tin, and pinched bottles of champagne from her father's wine cellar. She still lived at home in the suburbs with her widowed daddy, retired from his insurance job, whom she adored – though Ann thought he was a horrible old man. He'd told her once that little tarts ought to be flogged, to teach them a lesson.

They drank his champagne anyway, from eighteenth-century glasses, which they'd brought from the house because Blaise couldn't find anything else. When the champagne was finished, Kit brought out a bottle of her father's Armagnac – I won't half be in trouble, she said. And somehow that afternoon they achieved the miraculous drunkenness you only get once or twice in a lifetime, brilliant and without consequences, not peaking and subsiding but running weightlessly on and on. Afterwards Ann could hardly remember any subject they'd talked about, or what had seemed so clever or so funny. When they wandered in the grounds in the evening, after the public had gone, Nola took off her black shoes and walked carefree in her stockings. And Donny Ross's pursuit of Ann was as intent and tense as a stalking cat's: invisible to everyone else, it seemed to her to flash through all the disparate, hazy successive phases of the afternoon like a sparking, dangerous live wire. They lay close together but not touching, in the long grass under a tall ginkgo tree, whose leaves were shaped like exquisite tiny paddles, translucent bright grass-green. The light faded in the sky to a deep turquoise and the peacocks came to roost in the tree above them, clotted lumps of darkness, with their long tails hanging down like bell pulls.

Their drunkenness ought to have ended in some shame or disaster – Ray had drunk as much as the rest of them, and he was driving them home – but it didn't. They didn't break any of the lovely glasses etched with vine leaves; no one threw up or said anything unforgivable; no one was killed. They didn't even feel too bad the next day. Ray delivered the girls decorously back, eventually, to the doorsteps of their respective houses in Fishponds and Stoke Bishop. On the way home, Kit said what a sweetheart Blaise was – and what a fabulous place, imagine landing that! Didn't Ann just wish she'd got to him first, before Nola Higgins? Then Ann, with her drunken special insight, said that Blaise wasn't really what he seemed. He wasn't actually very easy. He'd seen right through them and he didn't like them very much. He saw how they condescended to Nola, even if Nola didn't see it. Kit said indignantly that she'd never condescended to anybody in her life.

They had not, after all, gone back inside Thwaite House to look in the cedarwood presses. No one had had any appetite, in the intensity of their present, for the past. When they had parted finally, because the medics were on night duty and had to get back, they had all made passionate promises to return. The next

211

time they came, Blaise said, he would show them every-thing. They couldn't wait, they told him. Soon. That was in 1953.

When Sally Ross was sixteen, in 1972, her mother, Ann, made her a jacket out of an old length of silk brocade, embroidered with flowers. The white brocade had been around since Sally could remember, folded in a cupboard along with all the other pieces of fabric that might be used sometime, for something or other. Now they decided to dye it purple. This was the same summer that Sally's father, the doctor, had moved out to live with another woman. Ann had sold all his jazz records and chopped his ties into bits with her dress-making scissors, then burned them in the garden. Of course, Sally and her sisters and brother were on their mother's side. Still, they were shocked by something so vengeful and flaunting which they'd never before imagined as part of her character. Her gestures seemed drawn from a different life to the one they'd had so far, where things had been mostly funny and full of irony.

Sally and her mother were absorbed together that summer in projects of transformation, changing their clothes or their rooms or themselves. Sally stood over the soup of murky cold-dye in the old washing-up bowl, watching for the blisters of fabric to erupt above the surface, prodding them down with the stained handle of a wooden spoon, feeling hopeful in spite of every-thing. She wasn't beautiful like her mother, but Ann made her feel that there was a way round that. Ann always had a plan – and Sally yielded to the gifted, forceful hands that came plucking at her eyebrows or twisting up her hair, whipping the tape measure around her waistline. The jacket was a success: Sally wore it a lot, unbuttoned over T-shirts and jeans. They both dieted, and her mother lost a stone; she'd never looked so lovely. Ann got a babysitter and went out to parties with spare knickers and a toothbrush in her handbag, but came home alone. At the end of the summer their father moved back in again.

Sally had always known that the white brocade had belonged to a lady who died before her wedding. The man she was meant to marry had owned a stately home with a deer park, and the twist in the story was that she'd been a nurse, had saved his life when he was ill. Ann and Kit Seaton – who was Sally's godmother – had picnicked with them once in the deer park. Then the nurse had caught diphtheria from one of her patients and was dead within a week. Her fiancé had written to them, returning their designs and saying that he would not need their services after all 'for the saddest of reasons'. They hadn't known what to do with the fabric, Ann said. They couldn't just post it to him. They hadn't even sent a note – they couldn't think what words to use, they were too young. Ann hadn't kept his letter or her designs; she regretted now that she'd hardly kept anything when she got married and she and Kit gave up the business. There were only a few woven Gallagher and Seaton labels, tangled in a snarled mass of thread and bias binding and rickrack braid in her work basket. She and Kit had never even thought to take photographs of all the clothes they'd made.

One weekend that summer Sally found herself at the very scene of her mother's stories, Thwaite Park, which was now used as a teacher-training college. Sally's boyfriend was an art student, and he worked part-time for a company that did the catering for conferences and receptions; she helped out when they needed extra staff. She wore her jacket to Thwaite deliberately, and hung it up on a hook in the kitchen. Her job that day was mostly behind the scenes, washing plates and cups and cutlery in a deep Belfast sink, while the hot-water urn wheezed and gurgled through its cycles. The kitchen was as dark as a cave, its cream-painted walls greenish with age, erupting in mineral crusts.

After the conference lunch, in a lull while the teachers drank coffee outside in the sunshine, Sally wandered upstairs to look around. Although the rooms of the house had been converted into teaching spaces, with bookshelves and blackboards and overhead projectors, you could see that it had been a home once. One of the rooms was papered with Chinese wallpaper, pale blue, patterned with birds and bamboo leaves. In another room, polished wood cupboards were built in from floor to ceiling; these were full of stationery supplies and art materials. Someone from the catering staff – not her boyfriend but another boy who worked with them, better-looking and more dangerous – had followed Sally upstairs, and she found herself explaining the whole situation to him – about her parents separating and the jacket and her mother's sad association with the house. Sally was trying her power out on this boy; she shed tears of self-pity, until he put his arms around her and kissed her. And then, amid all the complications and adjustments that ensued, she forgot to collect her jacket when they left, though she didn't confess this to her mother until months later. A jacket hardly mattered, in the scheme of things.

SK- 06/4/22